Murder at Hockey Camp

Roy MacGregor

An M&S Paperback Original from
McClelland & Stewart Inc.
The Canadian Publishers

An M&S Paperback Original from
McClelland & Stewart Inc.

Copyright © 1997 by Roy MacGregor

All rights reserved. The use of any part of this publication
reproduced, transmitted in any form or by any means, electronic,
mechanical, photocopying, recording, or otherwise, or stored in
a retrieval system, without the prior written consent of the
publisher – or, in case of photocopying or other reprographic
copying, a licence from the Canadian Copyright Licensing
Agency – is an infringement of the copyright law.

Canadian Cataloguing in Publication Data
MacGregor, Roy, 1948–
    Murder at hockey camp

(The Screech Owls series)
"An M&S paperback original."
ISBN 0-7710-5629-x

I. Title. II. Series: MacGregor, Roy, 1948–   .
The Screech Owls series.

PS8575.G84M87 1996   jC813'.54   C96-932019-1
PZ7.M4Mu 1996

Cover illustration by Gregory C. Banning
Typesetting by M&S, Toronto

Printed and bound in Canada

McClelland & Stewart Inc.
The Canadian Publishers
481 University Avenue
Toronto, Ontario
M5G 2E9

3 4 5   01 00 99 98

For Clyde Armstrong,
a teacher who made the difference

ACKNOWLEDGEMENTS

The author is grateful to Doug Gibson, who thought up this series, and to Alex Schultz, who pulls it off.

1

TRAVIS LINDSAY SHUDDERED. HE COULDN'T HELP himself. He had never seen – or felt – anything quite so frightening, so powerful, so absolutely raw.

The storm had broken over the lake. The boys in cabin 4 – which was known as "Osprey" – had seen it coming all afternoon: big bruised fists of cloud heading straight for the camp, the sky dark as night even before the dinner-bell rang. They had gathered on the steps of the cabin to listen to the growling and rumbling as the storm approached, and watch the far shore flicker from time to time under distant lightning.

There was a flash, and Nish began counting off the distance: "One steamboat . . . two steamboat . . . three steamboat . . . four steamboat . . ." A clap of thunder cut him off, the sound growing as it reached them. "Four miles," Nish announced matter-of-factly. Nish the expert. Nish the Great Outdoorsman ever since the Screech Owls' trip up North, when he nearly froze to death because of his own stupidity.

Then came the first overhead burst, and not

even Nish dared speak. Directly above them, the sky simply split. It broke apart and emptied, the rain instantly thick and hard as water from a fire hose. The boys scrambled for the safety of the cabin and the comforting slam of the screen door. Travis had his hands over his ears, but it was useless. The second crack, even closer, was like a cannon going off beside them. The air sizzled as if the thunder clap had caused the rain to boil, and the walls of the little cabin bounced in the sudden, brilliant flashes of light that accompanied the explosion.

Not even a half steamboat, Nish, Travis thought to himself. Not even a *row*boat between flash and thunder. The storm was right on top of them!

The six boys in "Osprey" moved to the window. Wayne Nishikawa in front, then Gordie Griffith, Larry "Data" Ulmar, Andy Higgins, Lars "Cherry" Johanssen, and, behind them all, Travis Lindsay, the Screech Owls' captain. They could barely see in the sudden dark of the storm, but then lightning flashed again, and instantly their world was as bright as if a strobe light had gone off. The streak of lightning seemed to freeze momentarily, like a great fiery crack in the dark windshield of the sky. Again they heard the sizzle of fire. And again thunder struck immediately, the walls bouncing, Travis shaking. He felt cold and frightened.

Another flash, and they could see, perfectly, as

if in a painting, the girls' camp across the water. Travis wondered if Sarah was watching. Sarah Cuthbertson had been captain of the Owls before Travis, and her new team, the Toronto Junior Aeros, were in six cabins out on the nearest island, along with the three girls – Jennie, Liz, and Chantal – who played for the Owls.

In the long weeks leading up to the end of the school year and the start of summer hockey camp, Travis thought he had anticipated every part of the upcoming adventure. Swimming . . . swinging off the rope into the lake . . . diving from the cliffs . . . waterskiing and fishing and campfires . . . even the mosquitoes. But he hadn't imagined anything like this.

The storm held over them, the explosions now coming so fast it was impossible to tell which clap of thunder belonged to which flash of lightning. It seemed the world was ending. The light over the lake flickered like a lamp with a short circuit. The rain pounded on the roof. The door rattled in the wind. And Travis shook as if he were standing naked outdoors in winter instead of indoors, in a track suit, in July.

It wasn't the cold so much as the feeling of helplessness, the insignificance. Being afraid of the dark was nothing compared to this. He'd gladly trade this unearthly light for pitch black and a thousand snakes and rats and black widow spiders and slimy one-eyed monsters lurking at the foot of his bed back home, where there had never, ever, been a storm like this one . . .

KKKKKKRRRRRAAAAACKKKKKKKKK!!

They saw a flash and heard a snap of thunder – but the sound that followed was new! It was a cracking, followed by a rushing sound, then a crash that made the cabin jump and the boys fall, screaming, to their knees.

"*What the hell?*" shouted Nish.

"*The roof blew off!*" yelled Data.

But it wasn't the roof! They were still dry! Andy Higgins, who was the tallest, was the first to stretch up and look out to see what had happened.

"Look at that!"

Now they were all up to see.

"What happened?"

"Lemme see!"

Travis looked out through the rain-dimpled window. One pane of glass was broken, and wind and water were coming in on their faces. Outside, the lawn had vanished. Across the grass, lying right between their cabin and "Loon," the next cabin over – where Willie Granger and Wilson Kelly and Fahd Noorizadeh and Jesse Highboy were staying – was a huge, shattered hemlock, its trunk split and its wood as white as skin where the bark had been ripped away.

It had missed both cabins by a matter of inches.

Travis began to shake even harder.

"THEY'RE COMING TO MURDER US!"

Travis woke sharply to two screams, one coming from Nish, the other coming from a chainsaw right outside the door.

There was light – daylight. Travis must have slept while the storm had passed. Nish was sitting straight up in bed, his sleeping bag pulled over his head, his arms wrapped around his pillow, and he was still yelling about murder. Travis shook his head: his friend had watched too many bad horror movies for his own good.

"They're cutting up the tree!" Travis shouted over the din.

Slowly, Nish pulled off his sleeping bag. He blinked in the bright morning light, then smiled sheepishly.

"I knew that."

It was amazing what a few hours had done. The rain and wind and clouds had all vanished. Sunlight was dancing in the wet grass, and the air smelled new and full of fresh-cut wood.

Two men, wearing hardhats and safety glasses and orange plastic earmuffs, were cutting up the big hemlock. Their chainsaws roared into the wood, the chips flying in a rooster's tail straight into their chests. The men were beginning to look as if they'd been coated in wet sawdust.

There were some spectators gathered off to the side. Travis could see Muck, the only one not in shorts. No one had ever seen Muck in shorts. He had a bad leg, with a long scar that Travis and Derek Dillinger had seen the time the three of them had gone wading after the keys that Derek had thrown away during the trip to Lake Placid.

Travis had trouble imagining Muck in shorts – in fact he had trouble getting used to seeing him in summer at all. Coach Muck Munro went with wintertime. He was at the rink when hockey season began, at the rink when hockey season came to an end. The players rarely, if ever, saw him in the months between.

It was almost as if Muck was something they pulled out of the equipment box in September and stored away again in April with the sweaters – all washed and folded, in his team jacket, baggy sweatpants, hockey gloves, skates, and whistle.

Muck was having words with a man standing on the other side of a thick branch of the fallen tree: it was Buddy O'Reilly, who ran the Muskoka Summer Hockey School, which included both the girls' camp on the island and boys' camp on the mainland. Willie Granger, the Owls' trivia expert, said Buddy had played three NHL games for the Philadelphia Flyers – "No goals, no assists, no points, thirty-two minutes in penalties" – but he carried himself as if he'd won three Stanley Cups. Buddy had on shorts, a tank top, and thongs. He was also wearing neon-purple wraparound sunglasses. And he was chewing gum, fast, using just his front teeth. He was holding a cellular telephone in his right hand, as if waiting for an important call, and had a whistle around his neck. His tank top had the logo of the hockey camp on the back and one word, *Coach*, stitched over his heart. He seemed to be laughing at Muck.

Suddenly, both chainsaws quit at once. A red squirrel seemed to be razzing them from the hemlocks that still stood. The workers laid the chainsaws down so they could twist a large branch. In the lull, the conversation between Muck and Buddy drifted through the cabin's screen door.

". . . irresponsible," Muck was saying.

"Nobody got hurt, big guy," Buddy O'Reilly said through the thin opening between his teeth. He popped his gum. "Nobody got hurt."

Muck stared fiercely, trying to find Buddy's eyes behind the mirror shades. He was very upset. Travis knew Muck would be furious at being called "big guy."

"Look at the core of that tree," Muck said. "It's rotted right out."

"And it's down now," Buddy replied impatiently. "It's down and nobody got hurt."

"Lucky for you."

"Relax, big guy. It's summer-vacation time, okay?"

Muck said nothing. He continued to stare, frustrated by the ridiculous sunglasses.

Buddy ignored Muck completely. He poked a finger hard into the numbers of his cellphone, then waited impatiently while the number rang.

"*Morley!*" Buddy shouted when his call was finally answered. Morley was the gentle, white-haired manager of the girls' camp. "*Morley! Get your butt over here! And find that lazy goof, Roger! We got a tree down between 'Osprey' and 'Loon.' He'll have to clear out these branches!*"

Shaking his head in disgust, Muck finally turned away as the workmen took up their chain-saws. He glanced over at the boys' cabin.

"*What are you staring at, Nishikawa?*"

"Nothin'," replied Nish. He wasn't convincing.

"Dry-land training at eight-fifteen," Muck said, and turned away.

The workers both pulled their chainsaw starting-cords, then gave the smoking engines full throttle. The roar made any more talk impossible.

The boys hurried to dress for breakfast.

The girls paddled over from the island camp for the dry-land training session. When they reached the mainland, they carried their canoes up from the beach and turned them over, stuffing paddles and life-preservers underneath. It was a wonderful way to start the day, thought Travis. Sarah paddled as well as she skated: smooth and elegant and strong. It was great to be all back together again.

Travis had been looking forward to this ever since Mr. Cuthbertson, Sarah's father, had approached Muck Munro with the idea of the two teams, the Owls and the Aeros, all coming to the Muskoka Summer Hockey School for a week. The camp covered an area the size of three schoolyards, the land falling away from the boys' cabins to the beach and dock, where they could swim and dive from a tower. A large boathouse at the far end of the beach held a speedboat and equipment for tubing, kneeboarding, and water-skiing. There were also sailboats and paddle boats.

The girls were on the larger of the two islands nearest the shore, and they were allowed to swim or paddle out to the smaller island, where they could hold marshmallow roasts. And best of all, at week's end, they were going to have a one-game, winner-take-all, Owls-against-Aeros Summer Hockey Camp World Peewee Championship.

Muck had never been too keen on the idea of summer hockey – "Ever seen a frozen pond in July?" he'd ask – but was finally talked into it by the other parents and the enthusiasm of the kids on both teams. Besides, the hockey school was just outside Muck's old home town, and he said he had a score to settle with a thirty-pound pike that was still lurking somewhere in the narrows that led out of the lake toward the town of Huntsville.

"This guy's a jerk," Sarah whispered to Travis when the boys and girls were assembled together on the training field.

She didn't need to explain. Travis knew she was talking about Buddy O'Reilly, who was indeed acting like a jerk. He had a new shirt on now – candy-apple red with the sleeves cut away at the shoulders to show off his muscles and a tattoo of the Tasmanian Devil chomping a hockey stick in half – and he was blowing his whistle and barking out orders. He had placed his clipboard beside him on the grass, and on top of the clipboard was the ever-present cellphone. No matter what the situation, Buddy wanted everyone to know exactly who was in charge.

"BEND! C'MON, BEND WHEN I SAY 'BEND'!"

Buddy had them doing warm-ups in unison: neck twists, shoulder rotations, leg stretches. Next he ordered everyone to do bends from the waist, and then, bent double, to roll their heads from one side of the knees to the other.

Nish fell over, face forward, which made everyone laugh . . . with one predictable exception.

"WHATSAMATTER, FAT BOY? THAT BIG GUT OF YOURS THROW YOU OFF BALANCE?" Buddy screamed at Nish. And though he wasn't laughing, he was smiling – delighted, it seemed, to have someone to pick on. Nish flushed the colour of Buddy's muscle-shirt.

Travis winced. *Fat Boy!* All Nish had meant to do was put a little humour in the situation. Travis had seen him do dumb things like that before, and even believed that Muck kind of liked Nish's hi-jinks, although Muck would never let on.

Travis looked around for Muck. He was standing off to one side, staring. Muck was the only coach the Screech Owls had at the camp – Barry and Ty, the Owls' two assistant coaches, couldn't take the time off work – and he seemed terribly alone here. Muck didn't have the camp personality. He just didn't fit in. He didn't allow any of the players to call him "coach" ("I don't call you 'forward,' or 'defence,' or 'goaltender,'" he once explained), and he didn't wear wraparound sunglasses, and he sure as heck didn't have any T-shirts with the sleeves ripped off them.

"KNEES UP! KNEES UP!"

Sweat was already pouring down Buddy's face. If this was warming up, Travis wondered, what was working out going to feel like? He could hear Nish puffing and chugging behind him. Travis didn't have to turn around to know that Nish's face would still be shining red. Only by now it would be from anger, not embarrassment. *Fat Boy!* What was with this guy?

At least Travis didn't have to worry about Nish fooling around any more. Usually, if Nish was standing behind you where you couldn't see him, you were in just about the worst place on earth. Just when you least expected it, Nish would be likely to reach out, grab the sides of your shorts, and yank down, showing the world your boxer shorts.

Data was so wary of Nish and his stupid pranks during gym class that he once took the precaution of joining his gym shorts and boxers together with safety pins. But the idea backfired. When Nish snuck up behind Data and yanked, the pins held all right – but Data's shorts and boxers *both* came down!

No, Nish wouldn't be risking another "*Fat Boy!*" insult. If anything, Travis thought, he would be plotting his revenge. And Nish was very, very good at revenge.

As the Screech Owls and Aeros worked out, a work crew moved the chainsawed logs from the cabin area over toward the tool shed. Travis could see a white-haired man struggling with one of the wheelbarrows. It was Morley Clifford, the manager of the island camp. Sarah and the other girls said he was a nice old guy, and Travis couldn't understand how he had ever got involved with Buddy in this summer hockey-school deal.

When the players had finished their field work-out, they ran cross-country around the camp: twice around the playing field, then up along the nature trail, down along the rock trail to the beach, and back, finally, to the main camp building where they ate their meals.

Travis ran with Sarah, and as they ran he wondered what it was that Sarah had been born with that allowed her to be so good at everything she did: skate, paddle, run. Sarah could even talk as she ran: "Word has it that Nish is planning the World's Biggest Skinny Dip."

"H-how d-did you hear that?" Travis panted.

"Data told me yesterday at lunch. It's all over the island."

"H-He's just k-kidding. You know N-Nish."

"He's nuts."

"T-tell me about it."

3

"SSSSHHHHHHHHHHHHH!"

Andy Higgins had his finger raised to his lips as Travis and Lars came back from the afternoon swim. He met them at the door, carefully holding the screen so it wouldn't slam behind them.

"What's up?" Lars demanded.

"Just don't say a word. Come on in."

The three boys entered the cabin silently, Andy carefully setting the screen door so it closed soundlessly.

Nish was lying on his bunk, flat on his back with his eyes wide open. His eyes were rolling around and didn't seem to be focusing on anything. Was something wrong?

"*Shhhhh*," Andy hissed very quietly.

Travis drew closer to Nish's bunk. His eyes were still rolling; he seemed to be searching for something. In his right hand he clutched the microphone from Data's boom box. Data had brought along the tape recorder and the microphone so he and the others could make up a camp song about the Screech Owls, but so far no one else had shown much interest in it.

What was Nish doing?

Andy signalled for Lars and Travis to freeze. Nish had raised the microphone and was holding it next to his face. Travis could hear a very quiet buzzing whine, and then realized that Nish's rolling eyes were following a mosquito circling around his head.

Nish hated mosquitoes. *What on earth was he up to?* Nish let the intruder land on the side of his neck, and, instead of raising a hand to crush the dreaded insect, he slowly moved the microphone closer. The mosquito rose, circled, whined, and landed a second time. Nish moved the microphone near again, causing the mosquito to take off once more. This time, when it landed, Nish's other hand came down like a hammer.

"BINGO!" Nish yelled, and rolled out of the bunk bed looking delighted.

"Did you get it?" Andy asked.

"I don't know," Nish answered. "I'm not sure."

"It's right on your hand," Travis pointed out. "You squashed it – look at the blood!"

Nish and Andy looked at Travis as if he came from another planet.

"Not the *mosquito*, dummy," Nish said, "the *sound*."

Andy and Nish settled over Data's boom box to rewind the tape. Then Nish pushed the *play* button and cranked up the volume.

Travis and Lars couldn't believe the effect. It seemed as if the cabin was filled with mosquitoes. The squeal of the insect was unbelievable. They could hear it circling, landing, circling again, landing, circling a third time and – *slap!*

"That's gotta go!" Nish said. Andy nodded.

"What's gotta go?" asked Travis, confused.

Nish looked at Travis, unimpressed. "The *slap*, of course."

"Why?" Lars wanted to know.

"You'll see, my friend. You'll see."

C-RACKKKKK!

Nish was first to jump up: "*What the . . . ?*"

"What was *that*?" Travis asked, running to the screen door. His first thought was that it was another round of thunder – or maybe another tree coming down – but the sky was clear and blue.

C-RACKKKKK!

"*It's coming from over there!*" Andy shouted, pointing in the direction of the shed where the lawnmowers and chainsaws were stored.

The boys began running toward the shed. They were joined by others heading in the same direction; the gang from "Loon"; Dmitri Yakushev from "Raven" cabin; Jeremy Weathers and Derek Dillinger from "Kingfisher."

Nish stopped in his tracks, his mouth falling open in shock.

There, behind the shed, Buddy O'Reilly was wrestling with a man holding a rifle! Buddy seemed to have jumped him from behind. The man, in greasy green coveralls, was trying to twist away. Travis thought he recognized the man, but couldn't quite remember where he'd seen him.

Others were running up now: Morley Clifford from the island camp, the lines in his face dark with concern; Muck from the cabins.

"What the hell's going on here?" Muck demanded in a low, cool, commanding voice.

Buddy now had the rifle free. He turned, triumphant, holding the gun away from the man, who scowled. Buddy held up the gun as if it were a trophy he'd just been awarded.

Muck moved faster than the Screech Owls had ever seen him move before. He ripped the rifle out of Buddy's hands, and worked the bolt back and forth to empty out the rest of the bullets – *one, two, three, four, five*, the bullets flew, spinning and glittering in the sunlight – and then he stomped them into the ground. Travis couldn't believe how smoothly Muck handled a gun.

"*Explain*," commanded Muck.

"Just keep your nose out of it, okay?" said Buddy. He seemed very angry.

"You fire a rifle around my kids, you answer to me," Muck said. "What's the meaning of this?"

The man who had been shooting spoke. He had bad teeth. "You wouldn't want a rabid fox around your kids, either, would you, mister?"

Buddy winced, and gave the man a look that said, *Why can't you keep your mouth shut?* Suddenly his manner changed, from nasty to nice.

"Roger here *thinks* we might have a small wildlife problem . . ."

Travis remembered where he'd heard the name. *Roger* – of course, the caretaker Buddy had called to clean up the fallen tree.

"Whatdya mean '*thinks*'?" Roger snarled. "You know as well as me there's rabies around."

"That true?" Muck asked, staring directly at Buddy.

Buddy smiled, but the smile seemed forced. "There *was*, but way back in the spring."

"A fox don't walk in here in plain daylight lest he's sick," Roger argued. "No matter what the season."

"Is that what you were shooting at?" Muck asked him. "A fox?"

"And I'd'a got him, too, if this lunkhead hadn't grabbed me."

"Easy now, Roger," Morley Clifford said soothingly. Roger seemed to respect Mr. Clifford, and nodded quickly, as if to say he knew he'd better cool down before he really upset Buddy.

But Buddy was acting sheepish, almost sweet. "C'mon, Roger. We can't have guns going off at a summer camp when there's kids all over the place, now, can we? Lucky for you they were having rest time in the cabins."

Roger spat. Travis could hear Nish beside him: "*Yuk!*" Roger obviously chewed tobacco.

"I think I know the difference between a rabid fox and a damn kid," Roger said.

"And I know the difference between a properly run camp and a joke," Muck said to Buddy O'Reilly. "You didn't think we needed to know there was rabies about?"

Buddy smiled, trying to win someone onto his side. "The Ministry said it was all cleared up."

"Not that I heard," said Roger.

Travis knew instantly that Roger was telling the truth and that Buddy was lying. There was something about Buddy's overly sincere look that told you not one word this man said could ever be believed.

"And you didn't think there was anything wrong with firing a gun with kids around?" Muck asked Roger.

Buddy gasped, shaking his head in disbelief. "You forget – *I'm* the one who tried to stop him from shooting!"

"It would all be over now if you'd just let me alone," muttered Roger.

Muck had heard enough: "Well, gentlemen – it *is* over now. I want the rest of those bullets."

Muck held out his hand. There was no mistaking the order. Roger looked at Morley Clifford – not at Buddy – and Mr. Clifford closed his eyes and nodded once. Roger seemed about to argue, but instead dug into the pocket of his filthy coveralls and pulled out a small box, which he slapped into Muck's open palm.

Muck pocketed the bullets.

"And I want a Ministry official out here to talk to the kids about rabies," Muck added in a firm voice. "Understand?"

"No problem," Buddy answered. He was smiling, but he didn't look pleased.

Muck looked at the rifle, now cradled in his elbow and disarmed. "I'll be hanging on to this until the end of our stay."

4

THE MINISTRY SENT TWO PARK RANGERS OUT IN THE evening. Both groups, the boys from Arrowhead Camp and the girls from Algonquin, gathered in the dining hall to listen to the talk on rabies. They learned what it was: a disease that causes wild animals to stop drinking water and eventually makes them go mad, often attacking other larger animals and sometimes even humans.

"You've all heard about the foaming at the mouth," the older ranger told them. "But that's when the disease is far advanced. There are few signs in the early stages – although the animal often shows up somewhere it wouldn't normally be. Like in your backyard, or walking directly toward you."

"Sometimes people get bitten and we can't find the animal to see if it really has rabies," said the younger ranger. "And unfortunately that generally means the person has to be treated, just in case rabies was present. That's a series of shots. Big needles, too, and they hurt – believe me, I've had them."

The kids shuddered.

The rangers quickly added that it was unlikely there were any sick animals around the camp. There had been a small outbreak in spring, but nothing lately. Even so, they said, the kids should avoid approaching any wild animal that appeared disoriented and not afraid of them, no matter how harmless and cute that animal might seem. They should be particularly wary, the rangers said, of foxes and, especially, skunks.

At the mention of skunks, everyone turned and looked at Nish, who had a reputation for making long road trips unbearable. Nish shook his head and rolled his eyes so he looked insane. He took a quick bite in Andy's direction and Andy jumped, which made the whole room break up.

Even Muck smiled. The Owls needed something to break the tension. This week at camp wasn't going at all as planned.

Nish had his own plans.

The boys returned to "Osprey" after the Ministry rangers had left and everyone had enjoyed a late-evening snack of hot chocolate and huge oatmeal cookies. Usually, Nish could be expected to beg or scrounge a second or even a third cookie, but this time he and Andy took off for the cabin as soon as the cookies were served.

They said they were wiped out and wanted to turn in early.

The others – Travis, Gordie, Data, and Lars – came in later, and already the lights were out. Andy was lying in his bunk, still awake, but Nish was already snoring like one of the chainsaws cutting up the big fallen hemlock. Andy raised a finger to his lips: "*Shhhhh.*"

The boys came in quietly, undressed quickly, and slipped into their sleeping bags. Out on the lake, a loon called. Travis smiled; he loved its strange, laughing cry. The moon was out, and enough light was spilling in through the cabin window for Travis to make out the bunks. He liked the moon coming in like that. No need for a night-light.

Travis could tell that Lars had fallen asleep. Data was also dead to the world; he was breathing deeply and, from time to time, mumbling to himself, but Travis couldn't quite make out what Data was saying. Perhaps he was speaking Klingon, as he sometimes did. Andy was still moving about. Lars was trying to get away from a mosquito. And Nish was still out cold. Or so it seemed.

Nish giggled.

Travis had been sure Nish was sound asleep. But no, he was moving in his sleeping bag, getting up. Had he forgotten to go to the bathroom?

Now Andy was getting up, too.

"What's up?" Travis whispered.

"*Shhhhh*," said Nish. "Just watch this."

Nish and Andy tiptoed over to the bunk where Data lay mumbling in a deep sleep. Nish kept giggling, and Travis and Lars crept up to see. Travis had no idea what was going on.

Nish pulled Data's boom box out from under his bunk. He hoisted it up and set it beside Data's head. "*Shhhhhhhh*," he repeated. It was hardly necessary, but Nish was now into heavy dramatics.

Andy balanced the boom box carefully and, on Nish's signal, turned it on.

Instantly, the room filled with the sound of a circling, angry mosquito. It sounded, Travis thought, as much like a siren as an insect, but Nish and Andy seemed to want it loud.

Nish pulled a white gull feather out from under Data's mattress, and as soon as the mosquito's whining stopped for a moment, which meant it had landed, Nish very lightly tickled Data's nose with the feather.

Data stirred, and Nish giggled softly, delighted with the results.

The mosquito on the tape recording took off again, the sound rising as it circled closer and closer. This time, when it landed, Nish ran the feather very lightly along Data's ear. Data's right hand came up and brushed away the tickle, but he didn't wake.

Nish signalled to Andy. Andy hit the *stop* button and then pushed *rewind*.

Nish reached under Data's bunk bed again and this time pulled out an aerosol can of shaving cream. Very carefully, he began to fill Data's right hand with foam. When he had built up a nice big mound, he capped the can and slipped it back under the bunk.

Nish gave Andy the thumbs-up. Andy pushed the *play* button and the mosquito took off again. Andy turned up the volume and moved the tape recorder even closer. Data stirred, mumbling.

The taped mosquito landed. Andy pulled the boom box away. Nish leaned over and poked the feather just under Data's nose, then ran it down over his mouth and onto his chin.

Slap! Data's right hand came up and smacked into the imaginary mosquito, sending shaving cream spattering into his face and pillow. Data mumbled, but didn't wake up.

"*Perfect*," hissed Nish, backing away from the bunk.

"Better than we thought," whispered Andy.

"Why Data?" Travis asked.

"Test case," said Nish. "Nothing personal."

"What do you mean, 'test case'?"

"If it worked this well on Data," grinned Nish, "think how great it'll look on our good friend, Buddy O'Reilly."

"Fat Boy" was going to have his revenge.

5

TRAVIS WOKE BEFORE THE MORNING BELL. IT WAS going to be a glorious day. He lay in bed, staring out the window and listening to the birds. He wished he knew birds better. He wished he could say things like "white-throated sparrow" instead of just "bird." He decided he would become an expert on birds some day. He'd even find out what an osprey was.

Data was sitting up in bed. He was rubbing his eyes with the back of his hands, but still hadn't noticed the dried shaving cream all over his face. He hadn't even noticed it on his hand. Perhaps it was too early in the morning for him.

"You feeling okay?" Nish asked with utmost sincerity.

Data blinked. "Yeah . . . why?"

"You don't look so good, you better go look in the mirror."

Data still hadn't caught on. Puzzled, he slipped out of his sleeping bag and peered into the mirror over the sink.

"*What the – ?*" Data shouted.

"You're foaming at the mouth, pal," Nish told him. "Looks like rabies to me."

"In-your-face hockey!

"You understand me – You, Fat Boy? – You understand what I'm getting at here?"

They were at the arena in the tourist town just down the road from the camp. Buddy O'Reilly was standing at centre ice, sweat pouring off his face. Nish lay flat on his back in front of Buddy, moaning as he gasped and twisted on the ice.

Buddy had just flattened Nish with one of the hardest and meanest checks Travis had ever seen, and the hardest, by far, he had ever seen at a "practice." The hit had caught everyone off guard, but none more so than Nish himself, who had had his head down as he moved up toward centre on a simple five-on-four power-play drill. Nish knew his job: pick up the puck behind the net, then lug the puck up past the blueline and hit Sarah as she cut across centre ice. He'd timed it perfectly, slipping a nifty little pass in under Buddy's outstretched stick and sending Sarah and Travis and Dmitri in toward the opposition blueline.

Then Buddy had struck. He hit Nish full on, his hands and stick coming up hard into Nish's helmet, and Nish had dropped instantly.

Buddy stepped back to demonstrate.

"You see what I mean by in-your-face hockey? This is what I want to see from you guys — I don't give a damn whether it's for the Stanley Cup or summer-camp practice. You take your man out. Understand? You okay, Fat Boy?"

Buddy was laughing — that strange, front-of-teeth, chewing-gum snicker — as he reached down and helped Nish get to his feet. Travis couldn't help noticing that Buddy seemed a little concerned; perhaps he realized he had hit Nish just a bit too hard. Nish skated away, trying to get the air back in his lungs. He was bent over, his face almost on his knees. His skates wobbled and he almost went down again.

Nish's face was twisted up and red. He was hurting, fighting back tears.

"You hit, you follow through. Understand? Hit high, follow through like I showed you, with your forearms — it's perfectly legal. You take him out, okay? You saw what happened. They came out on a power play, I hit Tubby here, and suddenly its even-up again, four-on-four, with Fat Boy wobbling off to the bench. Understand now? Huh?"

Buddy looked around, pulling nods of agreement out of some of the shocked Owls and Aeros. Others just stared, waiting to see what Buddy would do next. He had been screaming since the on-ice drills began, and he had skated them until Nish, predictably, had called out, *"I'm gonna hurl!"*

"Then Hurl!" Buddy screamed back at him.

It seemed to Travis that Buddy was particularly hard on Nish. Calling him "Fat Boy" and "Tubby," and now almost knocking him cold. What had Nish done to deserve this?

Muck had waited until the warm-ups were through before coming out. He had put on his skates and had his stick and gloves – his plain windbreaker a sharp contrast to Buddy's neon-red tracksuit – and he had stayed out of it, at first. This was Buddy's hockey camp, after all.

But after the hit on Nish, Muck came forward, pushing through the shocked players and speaking, very softly, to Buddy.

"Can I see you for a moment?"

Buddy looked irritated, as if his train of thought had been broken.

"How's after practice?" Buddy asked.

"Only if it ends right now."

Reluctantly, Buddy skated away with Muck. They left the ice entirely, leaving the remaining drills up to the two young junior players, Simon and Jason, who were helping out for the summer.

"I'm gonna get that guy!"

Travis turned quickly. It was Nish. He had

skated up behind Travis and was still bent over as he worked on getting his breath back.

"I'll get him – I promise you that."

With Buddy out of the way, practice became fun again. Simon and Jason ran a couple of passing drills and then decided to turn the last ten minutes over to a game of shinny – A-to-Ls versus M-to-Zs. That put Sarah and Travis on the same team, just like the old days, and against Nish, who slapped the blade of his stick on the ice and announced for all to hear that neither Sarah nor Travis would score while he was on the ice.

Travis hadn't played with Sarah since the Lake Placid tournament. And he hadn't played left wing since he'd replaced her at centre. Derek Dillinger joined them on the right wing for the opening face-off.

Sarah faced off against Liz Moscovitz, who'd joined the Owls after Sarah had left for the Aeros. Liz, who usually played wing, had no idea what kind of tricks Sarah could pull in a hockey game. Simon dropped the puck, but it never even hit the ice: Sarah plucked it out of midair, knocking it baseball-style over to Travis.

"That's *illegal*!" Liz shouted. No one paid her the slightest attention.

Travis had the puck, and he turned back quickly, skating behind his own defencemen and dropping the puck to Beth, a member of the

Aeros, as he moved back across the blueline. She read the give-and-go perfectly, waiting until Travis had beaten Liz before flipping the puck ahead to him. He hit Derek across ice, and Sarah broke fast toward the opposing blueline.

Derek sent the pass to her – hard and accurate.

But it never got there. A big blur slid across the ice and snared the breakaway pass before it could snap onto Sarah's tape. It was Nish! He knew Sarah's renowned speed, and he had guessed – correctly.

Travis could hear Nish's giggle as he passed while still down on one knee. Nish hit Liz, who was coming back across centre, and Liz, without seeming to look, fired a hard backhand pass up to Dmitri, who was breaking down the right-wing boards. Dmitri was in alone on net, did his shoulder fake, and fired the puck high in off the crossbar.

Nish, the hero, lay flat on his back, pumping arms and legs into the air as if he'd just won the Stanley Cup, in overtime.

"He's never going to grow up, is he?" Sarah said to Travis as she looped past him.

"Not if he can help it," said Travis.

He could see Sarah smiling through her mask. She didn't seem in the least upset that Nish had outsmarted them. "Watch this," she said.

Sarah won a second face-off from Liz and moved the puck back fast to Beth, who waited just long enough to trap the wingers before flipping the puck high and over centre ice. It was obviously a play they'd worked on with the Aeros. So long as the puck went across centre before Sarah, she wouldn't be offside, and she was so fast she could follow the lobbing puck and almost catch it on her stick when it fell.

The play worked perfectly. Sarah snared the puck on her stick and skated toward the net as Nish backed up, ready.

Sarah skated toward Nish, then cut sharply in a quick circle that let her drop her left shoulder. Nish went for the shoulder drop and lunged with a poke check – but Sarah's stick and the puck were gone. She had scooped the puck onto the end of her stick blade as if it were a small pizza she was about to place in a hot oven.

Sarah flipped the puck high over Nish's head and flailing glove as he lost his balance and fell. Then she skipped over him and walked in on net, pulling Jeremy Weathers far to the right before sending a remarkable pass back through her own skates and straight onto Travis's stick. Travis merely tapped it in.

Travis rode his stick like a horse to the blue-line. He yanked the stick from between his legs and turned it on its end, pretending to sheathe it at his side, as if it were a sword and he a triumphant knight returning from the battlefield.

Then he heard Sarah scream.

6

TRAVIS TURNED IN MID-CELEBRATION, SUDDENLY embarrassed that he had made such a show of a totally meaningless goal. Sarah's scream had come from the corner where she had turned after her cute set-up. She was crumpled on the ice, and Nish was skating away backwards, pointing at her with the blade of his stick.

Jason's whistle shrieked as he and Simon raced toward Sarah. Travis skated over quickly as well, passing Nish on the way. He glanced with dismay at Nish, but he couldn't read Nish's look. Anger? Surprise? Shock?

Simon loosened the strap on Sarah's helmet, and Travis was able to get close enough to see that she was crying before Simon chased everyone away.

"Give her some air! C'mon, back off!"

Travis and the others skated back toward the blueline. Everyone looked shocked.

"What happened?" Travis asked Dmitri.

"Nish took her out. He hit her from behind when she wasn't looking."

"Nish?"

"I saw him."

It had to be true. Jason was ripping into Nish over by the penalty box. Even in the hollow arena, the rest of the players could make out every shouted word.

"*You stupid idiot!*" Jason was screaming. "*You coulda broken her neck. You can't hit someone like that when they're not expecting it!*"

Nish's answers were harder to make out, but Travis knew his friend's voice well enough to get the drift.

"I thought we were supposed to 'take out our man,'" he said to Simon.

"Who told you that?"

"*Buddy*. That's exactly what he said when he creamed me. Remember? Or don't I count?"

"He didn't mean like *that*, you stupid jerk. You never, *ever*, *ever* hit from behind like that again. Now get off the ice before we throw you off! *Get outta here!*"

Nish swore and slammed his stick on the boards so hard it shattered. As he left, he pulled the gate behind him hard, so the noise exploded in the hollow rink.

Travis didn't need to follow to know what Nish would do next. Kick the dressing-room door. Kick every bag and piece of equipment between the doorway and his locker. Throw his broken stick against the wall. Yank off his skates and throw them against the wall – better yet, strike the blades so Mr. Dillinger has to grind them down and rocker them again before a new sharpening. Throw his sweater on the floor. Throw his shoulder pads in the garbage. Throw his socks. Throw his shinguards. Sit and slump and sulk in his underwear until everyone comes in and sees how badly life is treating poor Wayne Nishikawa.

Travis knew Nish well enough to be almost certain he regretted his check on Sarah the moment he realized what he had done. The problem with Nish was that he couldn't put the brakes on even when he knew he should – even when he *wanted* to. Having made the dumb hit, he had to follow through, knowing that only he would lose in the end. He was like fireworks. Once the fuse had been lit, there was no way to prevent the explosion. You couldn't change direction, delay, or stop. You could only wait for it to go off and eventually die down on its own.

Sarah was still lying motionless on the ice. Simon had done the right thing by not taking off her helmet or attempting in any way to move her. They were asking her about her limbs – "Your left foot? . . . Your right arm? . . . Wiggle your fingers for us" – and Sarah was able to do as they requested.

"I think I'm all right," she said. Her voice sounded weak and frightened.

"We have to be sure," Simon told her. "Jason's

calling an ambulance. You just stay exactly where you are and don't move."

Simon rose from his knee and turned toward the rest of the players.

"Practice is over for today!" he called. "Off with your gear and shower. We're headed back to the camp at ten-thirty sharp. Get a move on!"

Nish was exactly as Travis had pictured him: slumped against the wall, the results of his personal tornado all about him. He seemed distraught and angry at the same time. He was shaking his head and mumbling to himself. Travis figured it was just as well they couldn't make out what he was saying.

Everyone gave Nish a wide berth. Apart from Andy Higgins, hardly anyone even looked in his direction.

"That was a dumb thing to do," Andy said directly to Nish.

Travis was surprised Andy would be so blunt. But good for Andy – he was speaking for them all.

Nish made an empty-hands gesture to show his own surprise. "Fine," he said, his voice cracking. "It's a big joke when 'Fat Boy' gets creamed by 'Buddy Boy,' but it's a criminal act when 'Fat Boy' does the same thing to someone else."

"Don't be stupid, Nish," said Andy. "You didn't get hit from behind. And besides, nobody thought it was a big joke when that ass creamed you."

"I was just finishing my check," said Nish. He looked around, desperate for an ally, begging for anyone to agree with him, or even nod in sympathy.

"You may have finished Sarah," said Travis.

Nish turned quickly, hurt and anger flashing in his eyes. He hadn't figured Travis, his best friend, would turn on him.

"It was an accident."

"No it wasn't," said Dmitri. "It was just stupid."

Nish answered by picking up the one piece of equipment still within reach, a dropped glove, and hurling it hard against the ceiling. The glove popped back down and bounced off the top of the door to the washroom stall – up, over, and *splash!*, directly into the toilet boil.

The sound was so unexpected, the bounce such a fluke, that everyone in the room began to giggle. Nish had accidentally released the tension that had built throughout this disastrous practice, and the giggles became laughs, and the laughs became howls of derision, all aimed his way.

Nish slumped deeper into the bench, his arms folded defiantly, his eyes closed, and, it seemed, small tears squeaking out on each side.

The fireworks were over.

7

AFTER THEY HAD DRESSED, THE SCREECH OWLS AND the Aeros gathered at the edge of the parking lot to watch the ambulance come and take Sarah away. They stood in silence, not knowing what to say, not wanting to say anything, only hoping that everything would be all right.

Travis stood outside with Data and Wilson and Derek and Lars, the five of them with their hands in their pockets, kicking at loose stones with their sandals. They stared as the ambulance drew up, lights flashing. It backed through the Zamboni entrance and into the arena, right onto the ice and over to the corner where Sarah was still flat on her back, not moving a muscle.

Travis noticed Nish in the parking lot at the far end of the arena. He was leaning into the wall. He seemed lost. As Nish's best friend, Travis knew that now, only now, he should go to him. And if Nish felt like talking, they would talk. If he didn't, they would say nothing. Travis didn't have to hear the words to know how his friend felt.

He broke away from the waiting crowd and

walked toward Nish. He came up behind him quietly, but not quietly enough. Just as Travis cleared his throat to speak, Nish raised his hand behind him in a warning to be quiet. He turned quickly, finger raised: "*Shhhhhhh . . .*"

Travis tucked in tight to the wall. "*What's up?*" he whispered.

"*Take a look – but don't let them see you.*"

Travis poked his head out just far enough that he could see around the corner and into the arena's main parking lot. Beyond the two buses that would take the players back to camp was a flashy red-and-black 4x4: Buddy O'Reilly's truck, with his name on the side. Beyond the truck stood Buddy and Muck, toe to toe, arguing about something.

"*What're they saying?*" Travis asked Nish.

"I can only make out a few things. Muck told him if he ever so much as touches one of us again, he'll come after him."

Buddy was swearing now, very loudly. The words cut across the parking lot. Muck would not take well to this. He himself hardly ever swore. He threw kids off the ice if they swore. He made parents leave the stands when they swore at referees. Buddy was insulting Muck in a way they could never have imagined.

". . . *washed-up old fart!*" Buddy screamed.

He swore and yelled at Muck worse than he'd

yelled at Nish. "*The game has passed you by!*" he shouted. The disgust in Buddy's voice was cruel. ". . . *a bunch of losers coached by a loser!*"

Muck took a step forward and slapped Buddy's face. The slap was so hard, Travis could hear it as plainly as he heard Nish's stick when he had slammed it into the boards.

"*Did you see that?*" Nish asked. His voice was shaking with admiration for Muck.

"*See* it?" Travis said. "Did you *hear* it?"

Buddy recoiled in shock. He put his hand to his mouth and looked for blood, then threw his wraparound sunglasses in on the seat of his 4x4 and attacked. He lunged at Muck, but never got there. The Zamboni driver and Jason, the junior coach, had come running out into the parking lot and were trying to break the fight up before it started. Jason had Buddy pushed back toward his truck, and the Zamboni driver had his arms circled around Muck, who was putting up no resistance. Muck had made his point.

Buddy was another matter. He was struggling, but not too much. He seemed to be desperate to get back at Muck but unable to break free of Jason's hold. Travis had seen this a hundred times before in NHL games. The fighters made it look as if they were trying to get through the linesman, but in fact they were grateful the linesman was there and that the fight was over. You struggled for show. You made it seem like you'd kill the guy if you could only get there – a huge, hulking hockey player in full equipment, held back by a smaller, older linesman wearing hardly any protective equipment at all.

Travis wondered whether professional hockey fighters had any idea how silly this looked.

That's how Buddy O'Reilly looked now. He was much bigger and stronger than Jason, but he was acting as if he couldn't get through him. Travis and Nish knew why. "*He's afraid of Muck*," said Nish. "*The bully's a big chicken.*"

Buddy wouldn't throw a punch, but he was sure throwing insults.

"*You stay the hell out of my way!*"

The boys had to strain to hear Muck. "No, mister," Muck was saying in his steady, firm, almost quiet voice, "you stay out of mine if you know what's good for you."

Nish was giggling: "Good ol' Muck."

"Buddy O'Reilly's a nut," said Travis. "This thing isn't over yet."

Sarah Cuthbertson was fine. As she lay on the ice, they had locked her head into place with a special brace, then worked a stretcher under her and whisked her away to the Huntsville hospital. She'd been checked over, X-rayed, given a couple of Tylenol, and then sent back to camp with instructions that she was to rest and be woken up every two hours to make sure there had been no concussion. She'd be able to go back on the ice the moment she felt like it.

When word went around the camp, it was as if school had been let out for the summer. The Screech Owls, most of whom had been resting in their cabins, ran around high-fiving each other and cheering. The girls from the island camp paddled over, and they all spent the rest of the afternoon swimming and skiing and knee-boarding and wakeriding behind the camp's outboard, with Simon driving and Jason acting as spotter.

The star of the skiing contest was, much to everyone's surprise, Lars "Cherry" Johanssen. He could not only slalom but could take off on the one ski. Cherry was also the best on the camp's new wakeboard, turning 360s as he took the wake, and twice trying a full flip, once success-fully and once landing smack on his head, which brought a great round of applause from the dock.

"How'd you ever learn to do that in Sweden?" Data asked when Lars swam back in after his fall.

"You think we don't have summer and water and fast boats in Sweden?" Lars asked.

"Do you?" said Data.

"Of course we do. But I didn't learn it there. I learned those tricks in winter."

Wilson bit: "*How?*"

"Snowboarding, dummy. You ever hear of it?"

"You do that there, too?"

"There's a lot more to winter than hockey, you know."

Wilson tried the wakeboard but couldn't even get up. Travis tried it and got up, but he couldn't stay up long. Nish insisted on being next.

"You can't even ski on snow," called Travis from the water.

"If the Swede can do it, anybody can do it," Nish announced. He was back in form. No one, Travis knew, was more relieved than Nish at the good news about Sarah.

Nish put on a life-jacket and sat down on the edge of the dock. He called to Travis to push the board in to him.

"*You're not going from the dock?*" Data shouted.

"Why not? Cherry did."

"But he's an expert!"

"He can do it, I can do it."

Nish got the board onto his feet with some struggle, then picked up the rope and gave the thumbs-up for the boat to head out. Simon put the outboard in gear and slowly took up the slack, then he gave full throttle.

The rope tightened, and Nish closed his eyes, and hopped off the edge of the dock. The board submarined, then surfaced, and up went Nish, to a huge cheer from the crowd, led by Lars. *He had done it! Nish was up and away!*

Travis stood cheering with the rest of them. He hadn't expected this of Nish, who usually frowned upon any activity other than hockey or trying to rig up motel TVs so the Owls could watch restricted movies. He was doing a pretty good job of it, too, leaning his body just as he had seen Lars lean, digging in just as Lars had done. Only Nish, being so much heavier, was throwing up twice the spray.

Nish turned sharp so that a thick curtain of water rose between him and the cheering spectators on the dock – then it seemed the water behind the spray simply exploded.

"*He's down!*" Gordie Griffith called out.

"*Nish fell!*" Data shouted.

"*Whale!*" Andy yelled.

With everyone laughing, Nish surfaced, lake water spurting from his mouth. He did indeed look like a whale coming up for air.

Simon turned the boat and brought it around. He and Jason were laughing as well.

"*You want to go again?*" Jason shouted at Nish.

"*See if you can get up from the water!*" Simon yelled.

"*I'll try!*" Nish called, choking. He began struggling with the board, but it was impossible. It kept slipping off and popping to the surface. Finally he shook his head. He couldn't do it.

"I'll swim in!" he called to the boat. Jason began pulling in the tow rope, looping it neatly around his forearm as he did so.

Nish began coming in, the life-jacket making it difficult to swim with much grace.

"THE TURTLE!" someone screamed.

Travis turned. It was Liz Moscovitz. She was pointing off the dock, toward Nish.

"THE BIG SNAPPER!" Jennie Staples shouted.

Travis couldn't see it, but it had been there earlier. The area under the dock was home to Snappy, a huge snapping turtle, its shell as big as a truck hubcap. Sometimes on a sunny day it would crawl up on a log. It was grey and green and had a huge head and jaws. Someone said a previous camper had once tried to knock it off with a paddle and that the turtle had snapped the paddle clean in half before slowly dropping into the water and down under the big boathouse where the boats and sails and life-jackets were stored.

"*It's coming right at you, Nish!*" Chantal Larochelle screamed. She seemed really frightened, genuinely afraid for Nish.

Nish panicked. He began pounding the water as he tried to swim faster, but the life-jacket slowed him down.

"HELLLPPPPPP!!!!"

Simon heard him and gunned the boat toward Nish, who was now churning up the water as he tried to reach the boat.

"*Look out, Nish! Look out!*" several of the girls screamed at once.

Travis was running along the side of the dock trying to find the turtle, but he couldn't see a thing. Liz was on the diving platform, so she had a better view, and she seemed to be tracking the beast.

"*He's right under you, Nish!*" Liz screeched.

Nish howled: "AAAAYYYYYYHHHHHHHHHHHH!!!!"

Travis couldn't believe what he was seeing. Nish seemed to rise up out of the water, almost like a whale breaching, and straight into the out-stretched arms of Jason, who hauled him into the boat, stomach first. Nish spilled onto the floor of the boat while his feet kicked wildly in the air. They could see him run his fleshy hands along his toes. *Was he actually counting them?*

Simon and Jason leaned over the side of the boat and peered down into the clear lake water. They were squinting and shaking their heads.

"He's gone!" said Jason.

"Can't see a thing," said Simon.

Liz leapt from the diving platform and splashed into the lake almost precisely where she had been pointing. How could she do that? Travis wondered. How could she jump into the exact spot where old Snappy had been seen?

Chantal jumped off the dock as well. Then Jennie, Sareen, Beth – all the girls from the island camp. And when they surfaced, they all were laughing.

There had been no turtle sighting at all. They were just getting a little revenge for their friend Sarah.

8

SARAH WAS AT SUPPER. SHE SEEMED FINE. SHE'D slept in the afternoon, and probably should have stayed in bed in the evening, but she didn't want to miss out on any fun. After they ate, there was to be a singsong down by the beach.

Nish stayed away from the gang gathering around Sarah's table. He was obviously still embarrassed about the snapping-turtle false alarm. But it wasn't just that: it seemed to Travis that Nish didn't know how to tell Sarah how bad he felt. He was acting as if the whole thing would eventually go away if he just waited long enough.

Travis was sitting with Sarah when the others went to line up for cookies. Jennie said she'd get one for Sarah, and Data was getting one for Travis, so the two Screech Owls captains, one former and the other current, were left alone.

"Are you mad at him?" asked Travis.

"*Nish?*" Sarah said, as if she couldn't quite make the connection. "Mad at him? How can you get mad at Nish?"

"Muck does."

"Muck only does it because he knows Nish expects him to. And he knows Nish won't stop unless someone stops him. But I doubt Muck ever really gets mad at anybody."

"He sure was at Buddy today."

Travis told the story of the incident in the arena parking lot.

"It's guys like Buddy that make people quit hockey," Sarah said.

"I think he's a jerk," Travis offered.

"You heard Roger quit, eh?"

"Roger?"

"The caretaker. Mr. Clifford told us. He said Roger couldn't take working with that idiot Buddy, so he just walked off the job."

"No wonder we haven't seen him around."

"Mr. Clifford told us he'd walk out on Buddy, too – if he could afford to."

"What's he mean? He could get another job at another camp. He's a really nice guy."

"He *owns* the island camp."

"I thought Buddy did."

"Buddy just acts like he owns everything. They're partners. Mr. Clifford's family used to own both camps. It was his idea to set up the hockey school. He says he needed a partner who knew hockey and had the right connections, so he threw in with Buddy."

"I bet he regrets that decision," said Travis.

The others came back with the cookies just as Morley Clifford stood up and rapped a soup spoon against a pie plate to get everyone's attention. He had an announcement to make.

"Boys and girls," he said, "if I can have your attention here a minute before we start the singsong..."

Everyone quieted down to listen. It was clear they all liked Mr. Clifford – the girls on the island adored him – and unlike Buddy O'Reilly, he never, ever, raised his voice. As the Screech Owls had learned from Muck, you didn't need to yell to get someone's attention.

RRRRIIIIINNNNGGG!

It was a cellular phone – Buddy O'Reilly's, of course. A groan went around the room. Buddy yanked the phone out of the holster on his belt and ducked out the door, seemingly grateful for the excuse to slip away.

Everyone booed.

Morley Clifford waited patiently for quiet to return. "... There was an incident today, I understand, at the docks."

A few of the kids snickered. Several of them turned to stare at Nish, who was scrunched down in his seat chewing on his cookie. His face began to turn the shade of the setting sun.

"I've lived all my life on this lake," said Mr. Clifford. "I have never seen, or heard of, a snapping turtle bothering anyone. And I called the

Ministry of Natural Resources this afternoon just for confirmation. There has never been an incident recorded – ever – of a snapping turtle biting a swimmer. They are big, beautiful, gentle reptiles. They can't move very fast on land, so they'll sometimes strike back if someone tries to hurt them. But in the water you have nothing, absolutely nothing, to fear. Are we clear on that point?"

Everyone turned toward Nish. As one, they asked: "*NNNIIIIISSHHHH?*"

Nish's face looked like a hot plate. He squirmed, then bit into his cookie, trying to act as if he was just one of the crowd. It wasn't working. Nish would never be just part of the crowd, no matter how hard he tried.

After the marshmallows and singsong they all gathered at the beach. The girls and Mr. Clifford were going to canoe in a convoy back to the island. The stars were out, and they looked magnificent. They had different stars in the country than they did in the city, Travis thought. Just as they have different traffic and different stores.

Mr. Clifford had a circle of campers around him. He was pointing out the North Star to them. "The bright one, there. You see the Big Dipper," he said. Everyone could see it plainly. "Just follow the line. See it now? Good."

He showed them Orion and the Archer and he pointed out the Milky Way.

"There are billions of stars out there," he said. "Not hundreds. Not thousands. Not millions. But thousands and thousands and thousands of millions. Think about it."

Mr. Clifford paused, and everyone thought about all those stars. Travis shuddered. He couldn't help it.

"Our own star is so minor as to be almost completely insignificant," he said. "And yet our star, the sun, has nine planets *that we know of* – and scientists have just learned that there was once life on Mars. Think about *that.*

"Now consider for a moment that it is very, very likely that every one of those billions and billions of stars has its own planets – maybe one big star has thousands of planets, who knows? Somewhere out there there is bound to be another planet our size and our distance from its sun, and maybe it's got a lake and a summer camp where they make huge oatmeal-and-raisin cookies."

Travis could hear gasps all around him. None of them had ever considered such a possibility. You looked up at the stars in the city, or even in a small town, and it was as if you were looking up at a ceiling with the odd tiny light in it. Nothing more. Nothing beyond.

"Or just maybe," Mr. Clifford continued, "life

up there is a mirror image of ours. Maybe things developed just a bit differently up there. They say snapping turtles are living dinosaurs, did you know that? Maybe up there the dinosaurs didn't die out. Maybe on this planet we'll call, what . . . well, why not *Algonquin*?" – the girls from the island all cheered – "the turtles are the hockey players . . ."

Everyone laughed. Travis had never heard such an imagination.

". . . and maybe right now they're running like heck to get away from the Snapping Nishikawa that lives under *their* dock!"

A huge shout of delight burst from Mr. Clifford's audience. They turned to look for Nish and howled with laughter. Why couldn't they have Morley Clifford on their side of the bay? Travis thought. Why did they have to have Buddy O'Reilly?

"Come on, now, Screech Owls," Morley Clifford shouted. "Let's help get these canoes in the water."

The Aeros and Screech Owls worked together. They turned the canoes and hoisted them down onto the beach. The girls put on their life-jackets and checked their paddles and began pushing out.

"I'm not afraid of any turtle," Nish said as they waded into the water with Liz's boat.

"Nor is anyone else – now," said Liz. She was still cool to Nish, not yet in a forgiving mood.

But Sarah was her old self. "What's this we hear about the World's Biggest Skinny Dip, Nish?" she asked.

Sarah had broken the ice herself. Grateful, Nish leapt with both feet.

"I'm doing it," he said. "Before the end of camp."

"You haven't got the guts," Sarah laughed.

"Have so," Nish protested.

"You do it," Sarah said, "and produce witnesses to prove it, and I'll get you an Aeros T-shirt."

Sarah knew exactly how to work Nish. He'd been begging for an Aeros shirt since he first saw them.

"You're on," he said.

9

TONIGHT WAS THE NIGHT THEY WOULD FIX
Buddy O'Reilly. Back at "Osprey" cabin, Andy
Higgins cut the blade off a hockey stick, then
straightened out a coat hanger and attached it
to the end of the stick with hockey tape.

"What on earth is that for?" Data wanted to
know.

"That's how we're going to turn on your tape
recorder, pal," Andy said.

"I can do it myself, thanks."

"Not in Buddy O'Reilly's cabin you can't."

How did I get myself into this? Travis wondered.

Because he was the smallest, he'd been
elected to place the tape recorder in Buddy's
cabin, which was just behind the main hall.
Nish and Andy had tracked Buddy down – he
was drinking beer in the kitchen with the cook
while the Blue Jays game played on a little TV in
the corner – and they kept up a watch, sig-
nalling to Data by the shed, who signalled to
Lars at the corner of Buddy's cabin, who kept
Travis up to date.

"*Still clear*," Lars would hiss. "*Still clear.*"

Travis thought his heart was going to rip right through his chest. He couldn't swallow. He couldn't talk. But he was doing it, not because he wanted to do mischief or because he felt any pressure to do it – but because he wanted to. He couldn't stand Buddy O'Reilly, and if Nish was going to get his revenge, then Travis Lindsay wanted a part of it for himself. He was actually enjoying this, even if he was scared half out of his wits.

He found the perfect place for Data's tape recorder: tucked out of sight under the steel frame of Buddy's bed, but close enough for the hockey stick to reach to turn it on. Andy had earlier cut a small flap in the screen with his jack-knife, so they wouldn't have to risk opening and closing the screen door once Buddy was inside and asleep.

Travis checked the tape to make sure it had been rewound, then checked the buttons to make sure the *pause* wasn't on. He had scooted out and away with Lars long before the signal came from Nish and Andy that Buddy and the cook had turned off the game. Buddy had drained his last beer and was headed for bed.

By the time Buddy shut the door to his cabin, the boys were completely hidden in the dark cedars that grew between Buddy's cabin and the shed. They had only to wait. The stars were not as bright now as they had been earlier, but they were still out in the eastern half of the sky. To the west, the sky was darkening. Cloud cover was moving in. In the distance, Travis could make out the odd low rumble: the sound of an advancing storm. Perhaps it would pass them by, but even if it didn't, it was still a long way off. They'd have time.

"I wish I had a smoke," said Nish.

"Somebody'd see the light," countered Travis. He hated it when Nish talked this way, trying to be something he wasn't.

"Then a chew," said Nish.

"You'd *chew* tobacco?" said Data, disgusted.

"Yuk!" said Lars.

"*Shhhhhh . . . ,*" said Andy.

Buddy's light had been out for some time. When Andy had got them quiet, they all listened as hard as they could. They could hear an owl in the distance. And every once in a while a distant rumble from the far-away storm.

"He's snoring," said Andy. "Let's go!"

They all waited a moment longer, just to be sure. It was snoring all right. And it was coming from Buddy's cabin. Andy scrambled out of the cedars, followed by Nish. Travis could hear Nish's breathing: excited, a bit frightened.

With the other boys trailing, Andy and Nish made their way to the cabin door. Buddy had shut only the screen door so as to let in the cool air, and they could make out his bed in the moonlight.

Buddy's mouth was open. He was dead to the world. His left hand was over the side of the bed, the palm wide open. Andy gave a hand signal for Nish to bring the stick-and-hanger combination. He was already pulling back the flap of screen that he'd cut earlier.

Nish attached a big soup spoon to the stick and piled it high with shaving cream. The can made a low, quiet *hisssss*. Very slowly, they worked the stick in through the flap. Expertly, Nish dumped the light-as-air cream into Buddy's hand. Buddy didn't even flinch. Working together, silently, Nish and Andy pulled the stick back out and removed the spoon. Leaning low, they could make out the shadow of Data's boom box, so they knew where to aim. With Andy steadying the stick, Nish lined it up and very gently, very carefully, pushed the button.

Quickly, they removed the stick once more. Andy fumbled for the feather to tickle Buddy's nose. He dropped it, and picked it up again. They would have to move fast. He began wrapping the tape around the feather's stem.

RRRRRIIIIINNNGGGGG!

It was Buddy's cellphone. Travis's heart almost flew through the top of his head.

The phone. The phone! The cellphone was ruining everything.

Andy and Nish scrambled away from the door and leapt back into the cedars after the others.

They could hear Buddy swearing through the screen.

"*What the – ?*"

A light went on.

"*Who the hell – ?*"

They could see him shaking his hand. He had grabbed the phone with the hand full of shaving cream, and now it was all over everything. The precious phone slipped and fell, crashing to the floor. Buddy cursed and grabbed it with his other hand.

"*Hang on! Hang on!*" Buddy shouted. "*Just a damned minute, okay? Some kid snuck in here and . . .*"

The Screech Owls didn't have to hear any more. They were already hightailing it back to "Osprey," laughing so hard they could hardly catch their breath.

Maybe it hadn't worked out according to plan. But this way – with shaving cream all over the phone, all over Buddy's ear, all over his hand, all over his room – the result was better than anything they could have imagined.

Whoever had made that telephone call to Buddy at that particular moment, *Thank you, thank you, thank you . . .*

10

"KKKKKK-RRRRRAAAAACKKKKKKKKK!!"

Travis sat straight up in his bunk, his eyes wide open. The last time he had been in this cabin and heard a crack like that it had been instantly followed by a rush of air and the crash of the falling hemlock. This time, however, there was only the burst of thunder, followed by nothing. He could hear rumbling in the distance; the storm was closer, but still not raining on the camp. The crack that had woken him must have been moving ahead of the pack. Travis lay back down in his bed and was soon fast asleep once again.

The Owls and Aeros practised in the morning. It was, by far, the finest practice so far that week. It was almost exactly as Travis had envisioned hockey camp would be. Muck set up the drills, and Jason and Simon ran them. Morley Clifford was there, and came out during the break with Gatorade and sliced oranges for the players.

The difference, everyone knew, was that

Buddy O'Reilly wasn't around. No fancy track-suit with his name all over it. No shrieking whistle. No chewing out anybody who failed to do exactly as he said. No picking on Nish.

They played a few games – even British Bulldog, which they hadn't played since novice – and then had a wild and crazy scrimmage, defencemen and goaltenders against forwards. The goalies and defence won by about a zillion-to-ten, because Travis's side had no one with the slightest notion of how to make a save.

Nish was the hero of the scrimmage. His puck-carrying abilities were the best of all the defence. He once even set up Jennie Staples, *a goaltender*, for a goal when he went in on the last forward back – poor Dmitri – faked him to the ice, and then sent a perfect Sarah-like pass back between his skates to Jennie, who was driving to the net as fast as her big goalie pads would let her.

After the goal, Nish skated over to Sarah Cuthbertson and went down on both knees, his head bowed. It was Nish's way of finally apologizing for what he'd done to her after she had made the same play the day before. Sarah knew Nish well enough to know how hard this was for him. She wasn't interested in any revenge that might involve hammering Nish head-first into the boards. She laughed, turned her stick around, and tapped him on both shoulders: Sir Nish, Knight of the Between-Your-Skates Pass.

Practice over, the happy Screech Owls and Aeros were on the buses to go back to camp, when Simon and Jason came down the aisle and leaned over the seat Travis was sharing with Nish.

"Good on you, Nishikawa," Simon said.

"Classy act, Nish — proud of you," Jason added.

Nish nodded and looked down. Travis could see that his friend was battling to contain a smile; he was looking straight down into his lap, trying with all his might to remain serious.

Sarah came along, the last player to board the bus. She, too, stopped as she passed.

"You guys ready for adventure?" she asked.

Nish looked up. "Whatdya mean?"

"Muck's given me permission to take you two out in a canoe to the little island this afternoon. We can swim and jump from the rocks."

Travis looked up, unsure. "It's okay?"

"Of course it's okay. I'm a fully qualified Red Cross lifeguard, you know. Nish goes down, I can go get him."

Travis smiled. "Would you *have* to?"

"Are you up for it?" Sarah asked.

"Sure," said Travis.

"Nish?"

Nish just nodded. He wasn't even trying to fight the grin any more.

Before they took out the canoe, Travis and Nish had to take care of their wet hockey equipment. They spread it on the ground in front of the cabin so it would dry in the sun. Travis noticed there wasn't even a light dew on the grass, and he remembered the storm during the night. It must have passed right over the camp without raining. He wondered if the lightning with the single clap of thunder had struck anything.

"Let's go!" Nish shouted.

Nish was excited. Before he'd come to camp, he'd never even been in a canoe. Now he thought that, next to Sea-doos – and anything else that had an outboard engine, for that matter – canoes were a terrific way to move about the water. Like the others, he thought the silence was incredible, the way they could sneak up on almost anything: the loons, the ducks, maybe even old Snappy sitting out sunning on a log.

The two boys ran across the main camp grounds and down along the beach to the boathouse. Sarah was already there, waiting for them.

"I thought maybe you'd chickened out," she said.

"You seem to forget you knighted me," said Nish. "I'm ready for anything – even hand-to-hand combat with that stupid turtle."

"*Right*," Sarah laughed.

Nish was anxious to get going. He opened the

door to the boathouse and the three friends entered. Inside, the air was musty from woodrot and years of wet life-preservers. But it also smelled neat. The walls had never been painted, and there was the faint odour of cedar, and of oil and gas and outboards – the smells of summer at the lake. They could hear the waves lapping lightly under the boat slip. A swallow left its nest high in the beams and swooped out under the main door.

There were two canoes in the boathouse. One was missing a stern seat, so they moved out the good one and began loading up. Sarah had even brought a small picnic for them.

"I'll get the paddles," offered Travis.

He looked around: old fishing rods, sails, rudders, oars, a fibreglass canoe with a great gaping hole in its side, an auger for drilling holes in the ice on the lake in winter, several old propane lamps that needed cleaning, water-skis, the tube, a new wakeboard.

"Over there!" Sarah called to him.

She was pointing to a jumble of ropes and stacked-up gas tanks on the far side of the slip.

Travis jumped across the slip, took one step, and crashed down onto the rough boards.

"*Walk much?*" Nish shouted. He was laughing.

"You okay, Trav?" Sarah called.

"I slipped on something," Travis answered. He felt okay. He wasn't hurt. He had put his arm down to break his fall, and something had jabbed him near the wrist. "There was something here on the boards," he said, struggling up.

"Yeah," laughed Nish. "Your own shadow!"

Travis bent down to look. It was difficult to see. He rubbed his arm. Whatever it was he'd landed on was hard. A short distance away, something was shining in the dim light of the boathouse. He crept over and picked it up. Without a word he held it out in the palm of his hand for the others to see.

Sarah caught her breath. "*A bullet?*"

It wasn't a live bullet, it was an empty shell. It had been fired. Travis sniffed it: he could smell gunpowder.

Could this have been the crack of thunder that woke him up last night?

"*What's that on your arm?*" said Nish. He was pointing at Travis's other arm, not the one that had landed on the shell. Travis felt it.

Goo!

"What is it?" Sarah asked. She seemed concerned.

"I don't know," Travis said.

"Maybe that bird we scared out left you a present." Nish giggled. He didn't seem in the least concerned.

"It's pitch," said Sarah. "Pitch from the boards."

"I guess," said Travis.

There was a rag near the gas cans. He picked it

up and wiped his arm. Whatever the goo was, it was sticky. Probably pitch. He rubbed hard and got most of it off.

"*Let's get going!*" Nish called. "*Day's a-wasting!*"

Travis carried the paddles over to the canoe. Nish was already in, and Sarah handed him the waterproof bag with the sandwiches and drinks.

"We're short two life-preservers," Sarah noted.

"We don't need them," Nish said. He already had one on and was keen to get going.

"We're not going anywhere if we don't all have one," said Sarah.

"Okay, okay – but let's get a move on!" Nish said. "There's probably a couple over there where you found the paddles, Trav."

Travis went around the slip this time, not wanting to jump across and risk another fall. His arm was throbbing a bit. He'd have a bruise.

Everything was piled up in this corner as if it had just been thrown there – and yet everything else in the boathouse had been very neatly stored. It made no sense. He pulled away a couple of the gas cans, some rope, and a pair of old oars. He yanked at a plastic tarp that had been thrown into the mess. It was stuck, but he was sure he could see the faded red of a life-preserver underneath. He yanked again and the tarpaulin gave a little.

There was something sticky on it. It felt the same as what had been on his arm. It couldn't be pitch. What was it?

Blood?

He pulled again, and the tarp came free.

When Travis saw what had been hidden underneath, he gasped. He must be mistaken! The shadows . . . the bad light . . .

He moved so more light could get in. It was an *arm*, the fingers tightened as if trying to hold something. The arm went in under an over-turned canoe. And beneath the canoe, presumably, was the rest of the *body*.

"Hurry up!" Nish called.

Travis tried to speak, but he couldn't.

"*Travis!*" Sarah called sharply. "*What's wrong with you?*"

Travis stammered, then spit it out: "*Th-th-there's a b-b-body under here!*"

"*A what!*" Nish laughed.

"*What?*" said Sarah. She wasn't laughing.

Travis felt frozen, unable to move. He could see Sarah coming toward him uneasily. And he could see Nish scrambling to get out of the canoe.

"What do you mean a '*body*'?" Sarah asked.

Travis moved aside slightly so she could see. He heard her breath catch.

"Lemme see!" Nish shouted. He was scrambling across the planking.

"Wh-wh-who is it?" Sarah stammered.

"I don't know," Travis answered. He thought he did, though. He knew the jacket.

67

"*Move the canoe!*" Nish shouted. He was already pulling at the bow. "Help me!"

Travis moved without thinking. It was as if he was watching a movie of himself, stepping over and reaching down and taking the other side of the bow, and lifting . . .

Most of the body was in dark shadow, but as they raised the canoe higher, some dim light from the side door crept over its chest, and towards the face.

"*Buddy!*" Sarah hissed.

"*Is he dead?*" Nish shouted. He couldn't see as well as the others. The bow of the canoe was in his way, and he wanted to be closer to the action.

"I think so," said Sarah. But there could be no doubt. Buddy was white as a ghost. His face looked as if it had been carved out of candle wax. His eyes were staring past Travis, seeing nothing.

"Let's get out of here," said Travis.

"We better find Muck," said Sarah.

They set the canoe back down, carefully covering the hideous dead face of Buddy O'Reilly.

And then they ran, Nish well out in front of the others.

11

THIS WAS NO WAY TO PICTURE A SUMMER HOCKEY camp. There were police cars everywhere. There was police crime-site ribbon around the boat-house, Buddy's 4x4, even his sleeping cabin.

"Am I going to get my tape recorder back?" Data wanted to know.

Just like Data, Travis thought – from another planet. Who cared about his stupid tape recorder? He, Travis, had seen a dead body and he couldn't get Buddy O'Reilly's dead, empty stare out of his mind. He and Nish and Sarah were prime wit-nesses. They had found the body, and the bullet, and the blood. And Data wanted to talk about his tape recorder? *Give me a break*, Travis thought.

Muck and Morley Clifford had taken charge. They had called the police, and the police had brought along an ambulance. Men in white coats removed Buddy's body on a stretcher. It had been covered with a blanket when they carried it from the boathouse to the ambulance, but it was still a body. And everyone watching felt ill thinking that Buddy O'Reilly was dead, no matter what they may have thought of him alive.

"I saw him close up," Nish told the boys in "Osprey." Travis didn't bother disputing Nish's tale. He knew Nish hadn't seen much. Travis and Sarah had seen everything. But he wasn't about to start bragging about it.

Muck had phoned the parents in the morning. Some were already staying at campgrounds and lodges in the area, and they arrived immediately. Others were coming from down south.

Several of the parents had wanted to take their children away immediately, but the police said everyone was to stay where they were for the time being. They wanted to interview everyone who had been in either camp, just in case they knew something or had seen something, perhaps without even realizing it might be important. Some of the parents got angry about this, saying there was still a murderer about. But Sarah's father and Travis's father held a parents' meeting in the main lodge, and at the end of it everyone was agreed, if a bit uneasy, to let the kids stay on. The only condition they asked for was that police be stationed at the camp, and the police were only too happy to comply.

"Who do you think killed him?" Andy asked Nish when the boys in "Osprey" were supposed to be resting.

"I have no idea," said Nish. "Maybe he killed himself, for all we know. He could hardly have liked himself."

Travis shook his head. "There was no gun. Whoever shot him left with the gun."

"But there was a bullet," said Nish.

"Yeah, there was a shell."

"What kind?" asked Lars.

"How should I know?" said Travis. He knew nothing about guns. He didn't want to know anything about guns.

"Do you think you could ask about my tape recorder?" Data asked.

Nish threw his pillow at Data's head.

No one seemed to be organizing any activities, so the boys stood around with everyone else and watched the police at work. Men in suits went into the boathouse and came out carrying dozens of plastic bags, some seeming to hold nothing. There was a police boat drifting over the area between the island and the main camp, and two scuba divers were in the water.

"They're searching for evidence," Nish announced.

Travis shook his head. Anyone who'd ever turned on a TV set would know that, he thought.

One by one, the police were taking everyone who had been at the camp into the camp office and interviewing them. Two police talked to each of them, and another policeman wrote down everything they said.

Travis told the police his story exactly as he

remembered it. He had no idea who might have wanted to hurt Buddy O'Reilly.

"Did you see Mr. O'Reilly and anyone arguing or fighting in the past few days?" the older policeman asked.

"No . . ."

Muck! Suddenly the scene outside the arena, when Muck had slapped Buddy's face, flashed through Travis's brain. There had been a fight – well, *almost* a fight – and it had been Muck Munro, the Screech Owls' coach, who'd been arguing with Buddy O'Reilly.

Travis's voice must have given him away. The older policeman looked up from his notes. He cocked an eyebrow over his reading glasses.

"You're sure of that, are you, Travis?"

Travis squirmed. He felt sick to his stomach. He knew Muck hadn't done it, but he also knew he had to tell the truth. He had to tell the policeman every single thing he knew.

"Well . . ."

Travis checked later with Nish. Nish had found himself telling the same story. He seemed almost ashamed, as if he'd let the coach down, but Travis assured him that they had to tell everything. It wouldn't matter. The police would soon learn, if they didn't already know, that Buddy O'Reilly was an ass and that all kinds of people had words with Buddy.

"What about Roger?" Travis said suddenly.

"Roger?" Nish asked, puzzled.

"The caretaker who quit. He and Buddy fought over the gun, remember?"

"Yeah . . . *right!*"

They looked at each other, filled with confidence, then instantly filled with dread.

"But Muck took the gun away from Roger," Travis said.

"I know," said Nish. "I just remembered."

Travis decided he had better go and speak to the police again. They had to be told about Roger and the fight with Buddy. And if they had to be told about that, then they had to be told about the gun and where it had gone. But it couldn't possibly have been *that* gun that shot Buddy, could it?

The police already seemed to know everything that Travis could tell them about the incident with the gun.

"The rifle Mr. Munro took is missing," the older policemen told Travis.

Missing?

"Mr. Munro says he put it under the spare mattress in his cabin, but it's gone now. Do you know what kind of rifle it was, Travis?" the older cop asked.

"No."

"It was a .22."

It meant nothing to Travis. What was a .22?

"The shell you found in the boathouse," he continued, staring up at him over his reading glasses, "it was also a .22. Did you know that, Travis?"

"No."

Travis really didn't know what kind of rifle it had been, or what kind of shell he had found, but there was no doubt that the policeman was giving him this information in order to check his reaction. And what exactly was his reaction, Travis wondered, as the police excused him and thanked him for coming back with new information? He knew now that the gun Muck had taken away from Roger was a .22-calibre rifle. And he knew that a .22-calibre shell had been found in the boathouse. And as far as he knew, Muck had the only .22 around.

Travis felt sick to his stomach for about the sixth time in less than a day.

After he got back outside, Travis leaned against the side of the office building, catching his breath and waiting for his stomach to settle. A stand of pine and cedar grew close against the office, and Travis was hidden from the view of anyone approaching the door to the building.

A policeman walked up the path, carrying a long plastic bag. Inside was a rifle!

Travis stayed put. A window above his head was open, and he realized he could hear the voices of the men inside. The policeman carrying the rifle knocked.

"Yes, come in."

"Travers here, sir. The divers found this off the far shoal."

"A .22-calibre?"

"Yes, sir."

"Did you speak to Mr. Munro about this?"

"He just keeps saying he put it under the mattress in his room and that was the last he knew of it."

"What about the box of bullets?"

"Mr. Munro says that he disposed of them."

"*Disposed* of them?"

"He says he took them down to the dump the same day he took them from the caretaker."

"He says that, does he?"

"Yes, sir, he does."

Travis could almost feel the grin grow on the older policeman's face.

"Well, that's very convenient – but he may have forgotten one thing."

"What's that, sir?"

"We have a dozen witnesses who told us he ejected live bullets from that gun and then ground them into the earth with his heel. We find them, we don't need the box of bullets to see if there's a match."

"Yes, sir — I'll put some men on that right away."

"Good work, Travers."

Everything began to move so fast that Travis's head couldn't keep up with his spinning stomach. The police investigative unit set up behind the shed where Roger had fired at the rabid fox, laying out a grid of stakes and string and beginning to dig with small shovels.

Nish and Travis and Andy stayed and watched them search. They were there when the first policeman shouted that he had found something almost at the centre of the grid. With rubber gloves on, he picked up a bullet and dusted it off with a small brush. Another policeman brought a plastic bag over, the bullet was dropped in, and the bag sealed.

"Silver casing on the shell, wasn't it?" said Andy.

"Looked like it," said Travis.

"Same colour as the one we found in the boathouse," said Nish.

"Doesn't mean a thing," countered Travis.

But he knew exactly what it meant. He believed absolutely that Muck had tossed the box of bullets away. That would be just like Muck: they could have the rifle back eventually, but no bullets. He wouldn't have done it to hide anything, because Muck had nothing to hide. But what if the bullet they had just found matched the shell found in the boathouse? Only Muck had had access to those bullets, and now the police would think Muck had hidden the rest on purpose.

The boys watched the policeman dig up two more bullets. Each one was placed in its own plastic bag and carried away to the camp office.

Travis decided to return on his own to his window and see if he could learn anything.

"They're from the same batch."

Travis could make out the voice of the older policeman. He could sense satisfaction in the man's voice.

"The shell casing from the boathouse is an exact match with the three bullets we dug up. We'll need full forensic confirmation, but this is good enough for me. We have a rifle that someone tried to dispose of, a rifle that has been fired recently. We have a match in the bullets now, even though Mr. Munro claims he threw the original box of shells away. And we have the gun hidden in Muck Munro's cabin.

"I think, gentlemen, it is time to pay a call on our Mr. Munro."

12

MUCK WAS IN HANDCUFFS.

The Screech Owls – Travis, Nish, Data, Lars, Andy, Gordie, all the others – and most of the Aeros, stood around the parking area as the police led Muck away, in handcuffs. Travis's eyes stung. He looked at his friend Nish, and Nish was staring straight down at the ground, as if he was too embarrassed to look.

It had to be embarrassment, Travis told himself. It couldn't be shame. No one could possibly believe that Muck had shot Buddy O'Reilly, no matter how many clues seemed to point his way.

With a policeman at his elbow, Muck marched straight ahead, chin held high. The policeman tried to ease him into the backseat of the patrol car, but Muck stopped abruptly and turned.

He scanned the crowd. He stared, sure and steady and confident: it was the look the kids knew from the dressing room just before a very important game. Muck full of confidence. Muck with faith. Muck knowing exactly how things would turn out. It couldn't possibly be a bluff, Travis told himself. *Could it?*

Muck's eyes fell on Travis, and he stared.

Then he smiled, once, very quickly, before getting into the patrol car.

"He didn't do it."

Travis tried to put all the confidence he felt into the statement. He was not talking to the police any more, but to his friends: Nish and Andy and Data and Jesse and Lars. He wanted them to feel what he felt. Muck had stared at Travis because he wanted him to know something. He had smiled because he wanted him to know that they had the wrong person.

"Look," said Andy, "I'm as upset as anybody about this — but it doesn't exactly look good for Muck."

"He *didn't* do it," Travis repeated.

"How can we know that for certain?" Andy asked. "We *think* that — but we don't know it."

Travis had a thought. "But it was Muck who sent us to the boathouse. He wouldn't have sent us if he knew Buddy was lying there, dead."

"Yeah," said Nish, suddenly hopeful. "Right."

Andy shook his head. "Buddy's body was hidden. Whoever did it obviously figured he wouldn't be found so soon."

"He didn't *send* us there, either," added Nish, disheartened. "He just told Sarah she could take out a canoe. It was her idea to meet there."

Travis shook his head. "Muck didn't do it."

"He had the gun," Andy said, ticking off the points on his fingers, "and he knows how to use one. He had a fight with Buddy. He threatened him – there are at least four witnesses to that. And we all know Muck well enough to know that he must have hated Buddy O'Reilly."

"But not enough to kill him," Data said. "Muck wouldn't hurt a fly."

Andy paused. "Well, what would you think if you were a cop?"

"I know what you're getting at," said Travis. "*But he didn't do it.*"

"*Show me some evidence,*" Andy nearly shouted. He sounded exasperated, upset.

"There is none," said a disheartened Nish. "None in Muck's favour, anyway."

The boys fell silent for a while, each thinking his own private thoughts. Then Gordie Griffith, who hadn't said anything, cleared his throat.

". . . There's one thing," he said.

Travis pounced. "*What?*"

Gordie cleared his throat again. ". . . Who was there when Muck took the gun off Roger?"

"We all were," said Nish impatiently. "What's that got to do with anything?"

"Muck took the gun and pumped out the remaining bullets, right?" Gordie said.

"Yeah. *So?*"

"So how many were left?"

The boys all thought about it. Travis could see Muck wrestling the gun away. He remembered being startled at how familiar Muck had seemed with the gun. He remembered how Muck had aimed the barrel down, straight into the ground, before he pumped out the bullets. *One . . . two . . . three . . . four . . . five.*

"Five," said Travis.

"Five," said Data. "Exactly."

"Four or five," said Andy.

"Five," said Lars.

"I don't remember," said Nish.

"Your point?" Andy asked Gordie.

"Well," Gordie answered, "if we all saw five, and the police only found three, what happened to the other two?"

"Maybe the police just missed them," said Nish.

"Maybe they didn't. Maybe someone else came back and dug up two of the bullets."

"We better check," said Travis. He was trying to remain calm, but he couldn't help but feel some excitement rising. No, it wasn't excitement: it was hope. *Finally*.

The police had taken down the grid lines, but it was clear where they had done the digging. The boys got shovels from the shed and Travis found a screen that Roger must have built to sift earth. If they threw the earth they dug into the screen and shook it through, any bullet should quickly show up.

They dug for nearly an hour, but nothing.

"So we now have two missing bullets," said Data.

"The police will just say Muck came back and got them to use on Buddy," said Andy.

"Why would he? He already had the box. But it could have been someone who wanted to make it *look* like Muck had done it," said Gordie.

"What if he threw away the box before he decided he needed a couple of bullets?" countered Andy. "Then he'd come back here."

Everyone looked at Andy.

"Hey," he protested, "I'm not saying he did it. I'm just saying what the police would say to us."

"Look," said Travis, "we have to assume that Muck didn't do it. We have to give him the benefit of the doubt."

"Nobody wants him innocent more than me," said Andy, looking hurt.

"Okay," said Lars, "so what then?"

"Then it means someone else had to come and take the two bullets out of the ground."

"Okay. But who?"

"Who hated Buddy O'Reilly?"

Three of them spoke at once: "*Roger!*"

13

THE COOK KNEW WHERE ROGER LIVED: DOWN THE
road and past the dump, then the first place on
the left. A bit run-down, he told them.

"Isn't this something the police should be
doing?" Data wanted to know when Travis had
suggested they pay Roger a visit.

"The police have already decided who did it."

"They must have talked to Roger by now,"
said Nish. "What're we going to ask him that
they wouldn't already know?"

"I've no idea," said Travis. "I just know for
Muck's sake we have to go down there and have
a look around."

They took off after the morning practice – a
listless, dull affair put on by Simon and Jason
simply because there was nothing else to do.
Escaping was simple. They just opened a back
window in "Osprey" cabin, popped the screen,
slipped out, and cut off through the nature trail.

Travis appeared to be the leader. He knew they
were all looking to him as captain, but he had no
idea what they were seeing. A little boy desperate
to prove Muck was innocent at all costs? Or a new

Travis Lindsay, sure of himself and where he was going? Probably something in between, Travis thought.

He didn't have a clue where this road was leading them, apart from straight to Roger's place. They passed the dump, the stink rising high, the seagulls loud, and they came to the first turn to the left. It led to an old, run-down home. Out front, the sun was falling on a patch of bright orange irises that had grown up through the open hood of an abandoned Plymouth.

They thought about sneaking up on the place, but it was useless. The bush was too dense, for one thing, but there were also dogs in pens at the side, and already they were barking and jumping against the wire fencing at the scent and sounds of the boys coming along the road.

"We'll knock," Travis decided. He didn't really know why he'd said that. What alternative did they have? Turn and go back to the camp? Forget about the only lead they had?

"You first," said Nish.

"Okay," said Travis. He was captain, after all.

The dogs went crazy as the boys moved slowly up the rough laneway. They walked past an old refrigerator, past two huge truck tires that had once been painted white but were now flaking, past an old pump, and came to a verandah.

"Your idea," Nish said. "We knock or we run?"

Travis steeled himself. He stepped up to a wooden carving of a woodpecker hanging from the door, and saw that if he pulled the bird's tail its beak would hammer on the door. He yanked.

They waited a long time. A curtain moved slightly in the window closest to where they stood, and then the door opened.

It was a girl – a blonde, pretty girl about their own age. She seemed as nervous as they were. But at least she was smiling.

"Can I help you?" she said.

"We're looking for Mr. . . . . " – Travis remembered there had been a name on the mailbox – ". . . Sprott."

"That's my father," she said. "He's out in the work shed. I'll take you out there."

She led them around the corner of the house. The dogs were going frantic, trying to hammer their heads through the wire.

"You must be from the camp," she said.

"We are," said Travis.

"We heard what happened. My dad didn't like Mr. O'Reilly."

"Who did?" said Nish.

The dogs quieted as she approached. Travis realized that they weren't trying to get at them to kill them; they wanted to greet them. The girl ran her hand along the pens as she passed, the dogs lining up to lick at her fingers.

They came to the work shed and she opened the door. Her father, Roger, was sitting inside, painting several more of the woodpecker knockers that Travis had seen on the front door. All around were tiny wooden creations: windmills that looked like flying geese or Sylvester the Cat running on the spot; ducks and ducklings; old men and women who seemed to be bending down so their underwear showed.

"G'day, boys," Roger said. "What brings you down here?"

Roger picked up a cup and spat into it. Travis could almost hear Nish go "*Yuk!*" Travis looked at the girl and she rolled her eyes.

"We're trying to clear our coach," said Travis. He didn't know what else to say.

"There's a hundred people round here might take a shot at Buddy O'Reilly if they thought they could get away with it," said Roger. "I'm one of them."

Roger spat again. "But I didn't do it," he said. He looked at his daughter. "We were up fishing in Algonquin Park. Ain't that right, Myrna?"

Travis couldn't help but turn to Myrna. She was nodding. "We went camping with my cousins," she said.

Travis and the others looked at her. Myrna seemed sure of herself. She didn't sound like she was lying, and she certainly didn't look like a liar.

"The bullets Muck pumped out of the gun

when he took it," Travis said. "Do you know what happened to them?"

"Sure," Roger smiled. "Your coach ground them into the dirt with his heel."

"There were five of them. The police found only three."

"Is that right?"

"Somebody must have taken the others and used them on Buddy. That's why the police think it was Muck. The gun he took from you had been fired recently."

"Yah, but at a fox, eh?"

"The police would say it doesn't matter. They can't tell what a gun was aimed at. Just whether or not it was fired."

"Meaning?" Roger said. He didn't seem to follow.

"They think Muck took one of those bullets and put it in the gun and then shot Buddy. And we can't prove he didn't."

Roger took another long spit into the cup. Then he turned and looked suspiciously at Travis.

"What do you know about guns, son?"

Travis was caught off guard. "N-nothing."

"Any of yous?"

"Nope."

"Not me."

"No."

"No, sir."

"Well then, you boys can just relax. If that's what your coach did, they'll soon know for sure. And if he didn't, as you believe, they'll know that, too. The bullets can be exactly the same, and I guess that's what they're going on right now, but even if the bullets *are* exactly the same – same batch, same colour, same weight – and are fired from two different guns, they can tell. They call that 'forensic science.' You ever hear of it?"

They had, on television.

"You give the police time to do the proper experiments," he continued. "They'll sort it out."

Travis could feel new hope. He saw that Nish was giving the thumbs-up. Andy was smiling.

But Travis still had one question: "How come you quit?" he asked. It was obvious that Roger needed the job.

Roger eyed him carefully before he spoke. "I quit because I couldn't live with myself if I stayed on with that man. I know you mustn't speak ill of the dead, but Buddy O'Reilly was an evil, evil man. I seen the way he treated people. Didn't matter if you were a kid or a coach or a business partner, he treated you like dirt. And I won't be treated like dirt."

"Why did you work for him in the first place?"

"I worked for Mr. Morley Clifford, son. The finest man I have ever known. Mr. Clifford built both those camps into what they are. He only

88

took Buddy on as a partner because he needed someone who could run a hockey school. The only way camps around here survive any more is if they specialize. Mr. Clifford decided on hockey, which was a fine idea, but then he took on Buddy, which was a very, very bad idea."

"We thought Buddy owned everything."

"*Buddy* thought Buddy owned everything! He'd already cheated Mr. Clifford out of the main camp – the island camp was just a matter of time, the way I seen it."

"What do you mean, 'cheated'?"

"Mr. Clifford had to take out a bank loan to hire Buddy and get the hockey school going. But I have always believed, and will believe until my dying day, that Buddy O'Reilly deliberately kept the enrolment low at the hockey camp in order to put Mr. Clifford in a position where he couldn't meet his payments on the loan. When it looked like Mr. Clifford was going to lose everything, along comes Buddy with a couple of 'partners' he suddenly discovers – one of them's his brother-in-law, for heaven's sake – and they bail out Mr. Clifford. And who do you think ends up controlling the main camp?"

"Buddy?" said Nish.

"Bingo! You got it."

14

THE BOYS WALKED BACK TO THE CAMP IN THE midday heat, their hands in their pockets and their feet kicking up the dust in the road as they went over everything they now knew. The longer they thought about it, the more it became clear that, despite what Roger Sprott had said, it still looked bad for Muck.

They had barely turned into the camp laneway when Simon, half out of breath, came running up to them.

The whole camp had been looking for the boys. There was a big meeting about to get under way at the main building.

Mr. Cuthbertson and Mr. Lindsay were running the meeting. Standing to one side was the older policeman who had twice interviewed Travis. Everyone looked very serious. Travis had never seen his father look so grey and grim.

"Inspector Cox has a brief statement for us all," said Sarah's father, and even before the policeman opened his mouth, Travis knew it was not going to be good news.

Inspector Cox waved a piece of paper above his head. "This is from the forensic office in Toronto, where they've been doing ballistic tests on the rifle we discovered in the lake and the single bullet that killed Mr. O'Reilly. It's a match."

Travis's heart sank. He felt Nish's hand on his arm, tightening.

"In district court this morning," Inspector Cox continued, "a charge of first-degree murder was laid against Mr. Albert Munro."

None of the kids had heard Muck's real first name before. It almost seemed as if it wasn't him. But it was Muck, and it was hard to imagine worse news.

Travis was afraid to look at Nish. He was afraid they would both start crying. He looked, instead, to the far side of the room, where most of the Aeros were gathered with their parents. Sarah had her arms around her mother and was sobbing into her shoulder. Travis felt his own eyes tighten and sting and knew that a hot tear was rolling down his cheek. He didn't care.

Mr. Cuthbertson had something else to say: "Under the circumstances, the Provincial Police have told us we can now do as we wish. We think it best we close down the camp and head back home. You should return to your cabins to pack. Departure time will be six p.m., sharp."

The room emptied without a sound, apart

from a few sobs that couldn't be held back. Travis and Nish and the rest of the boys from "Osprey" walked back without a word, their heads down.

They passed by the main equipment shed and then by Buddy's cabin. The police had already taken down the yellow plastic ribbon that had marked it off as a restricted crime site. It seemed the investigation was over.

"I can finally get my tape recorder back!" Data exclaimed when he noticed.

Travis turned on Data, furious.

"*Get a life!*" he shouted. "*Do you ever think of anybody but yourself?*"

But Data was already running toward Buddy's cabin.

"*Jerk!*" Nish called after him.

15

THEY PACKED IN SILENCE. TRAVIS STUFFED EVERY-
thing back in his knapsack – pants, shorts, shirts,
sandals, bug spray, sunblock, flashlight – and gathered together his fishing equipment and his
hockey bag. The hockey bag was toughest. Every
piece of equipment he picked up and stashed
away reminded him of Muck.

Travis felt on the verge of tears. And all he
could think about was Muck sitting in a jail cell
somewhere, his big meaty hands folded in his
lap, waiting.

Data came in with his boom box. Travis had
to resist the urge to rip it out of his hands and
heave it down the steps. Data was thinking not
of Muck, but only of his poor tape recorder and
how hard it had been used.

"You wrecked my tape machine, you
dummy!" Data said to Nish.

Nish turned, shocked. "Whatdya mean,
'wrecked'?"

"You pushed the wrong button with that
stupid stick. You hit the *record* button instead of
play, and now my batteries are run down."

Andy pushed the *eject* button and examined the tape.

"You ruined the mosquito recording," he said to Nish.

"How?"

"Taped right over it. It's gone."

"Damn it!" said Nish. He snatched the tape from Andy and threw it against the wall. It bounced onto Travis's bunk, landing square in the centre of the pillow.

The *record* button? Travis's mind was racing. He leapt for his bunk, grabbing the tape before Nish could pick it up and heave it again.

"What's with you?" Nish demanded.

"*What if the phone call's on this tape?*" Travis yelled, holding it up over his head. "*Maybe it could give us some clues!*"

"Huh?" the others said at once.

"The call that came in to Buddy's cellphone," Travis explained. "It could all be here if Nish accidentally recorded it!"

"*Put it in!*" Gordie shouted.

"Batteries are all dead!" said Data.

"*Empty your flashlights!*" Travis commanded.

The boys rooted frantically in their packed bags and came up with enough batteries to supply the boom box. Travis put the tape back, rewound it, and pushed *play*.

They waited, the room heaving with their tense breathing.

The tape hissed, then they heard Buddy's cellphone:

"*Rrrrriiiiinnngggggg! . . . Rrrrriiiiinnngggggg! . . . What the – Click!* [the light going on] *. . . Who the hell – ? . . .* [a crash, the cellphone dropping, Buddy swearing] *. . . Hang on! Hang on! Just a damned minute, okay? Some kid snuck in here and . . .*"

Buddy's cursing went on for some time. The boys listened, picturing Buddy trying to beat off the shaving cream while keeping up the conversation.

Buddy didn't seem to have much respect for the person he was talking to – but then, Buddy had never shown respect for anyone. The swearing and contempt in his voice reminded the boys how much they had disliked him.

"*Now you listen here . . . I thought we were perfectly clear on that matter. You had until midnight tonight to meet those payments, otherwise the island camp is in a default position. . . . Just a damn minute here, mister, I'm talking! . . . You already know that my partners are more than willing to bail you out one last time, but in order for them to forward the funds to your bank account, you'll need to sign those papers I gave you. . . .* [a long pause, while Buddy listens] *. . . Morley, please, I don't need any of your whining right now. It comes down to a simple choice for you, the way I see it. You sign the papers, my group assumes control of the entire camp, or the island camp fails completely.*

Think of it this way, Morley, my friend: you sign the papers, you get to stay on. You don't sign them, you're out of business tomorrow morning. . . . [another long pause] . . . Fine, the boathouse at eleven tonight. . . . I'm glad you finally see things my way. This is going to work out just fine . . . Click! . . ."

The tape continued to hiss quietly, still recording after Buddy had ended the call. They could hear him swearing, still, as he wiped his hand and the cellphone clean. They could hear him moving about the cabin, probably starting to dress, and still cursing the kids who had broken in and filled his hand with shaving cream.

Travis got up and stopped the tape. They had heard enough. He walked over and hugged a startled Data.

"What's *that* for?" said Data.

"For thinking only about your stupid tape recorder."

"What about Nish?" Andy asked. "He's the guy who pushed the wrong button."

"I did it on purpose," Nish claimed. No one, of course, believed him for a moment.

"Who's Morley?" Lars asked.

"Mr. Clifford, dummy," Nish said. "The guy who murdered Buddy."

"The *suspect*," Travis corrected.

"C'mon – we have to get Data's tape to the police."

16

THE POLICE BROUGHT MUCK BACK IN A SQUAD CAR. No handcuffs – just Muck in his sweatpants and his Screech Owls windbreaker, and the same sure look on his face that he'd had when he left. The parking lot was filled with players and parents, and a great cheer went up when Muck got out of the car. Sarah Cuthbertson broke out of the crowd and raced toward him, hugging him around his big middle. When she broke away, his T-shirt was wet from her tears.

Mr. Cuthbertson made an announcement that the six o'clock deadline had been cancelled. They'd finish out the week. There was still time to practice. And, of course, they still had to have the big tournament, Screech Owls against Aeros.

"What about the World's Biggest Skinny Dip?" Travis whispered to Nish. "Is it still on?"

"Of course – even if the rest of you are so chicken I have to do it alone."

"You haven't the guts," laughed Travis.

Muck was swarmed by the parents, who shook his hand and slapped his back and generally embarrassed him. He seemed relieved to be back, but also anxious to break away from the attention and get back to being nothing but the coach of the Screech Owls.

The boys were headed back to "Osprey" when Muck called to them and came over.

They stood about, not knowing what to say to each other, and then, one by one, they all hugged Muck, and he hugged back. And after that, no one could speak anyway.

Mr. Cuthbertson had found out all the details. Inspector Cox told him that poor old Mr. Clifford had confessed everything the moment they played Data's tape for him.

The police figured that, under pressure from Buddy O'Reilly, the former owner of the camps had finally snapped. Mr. Clifford could no longer take the way Buddy was running things. They disagreed on everything, but particularly on the way Buddy treated the kids. He couldn't stand the idea of Buddy forcing him out and taking full control.

When Morley Clifford witnessed the fight between Muck, Roger, and Buddy over the gun, he saw his opportunity. He took the rifle from Muck's cabin, but he couldn't find the box of bullets and he'd had to dig up two of them from behind the shed. He never meant to leave that empty shell in the boathouse, but he probably couldn't find it in the dark. He panicked then, and decided to dump the rifle in the lake. He had been sure that Muck would have an alibi in case they found the gun and somehow connected the bullet to it — that way, the police would never figure out who had killed Buddy O'Reilly.

"It's a pretty sad story," said Mr. Cuthbertson. "The desire for revenge makes people do things no one would ever expect of them. But nothing justifies what he did. Nothing."

Mr. Cuthbertson looked at the boys from "Osprey" cabin. "It's a lucky thing for everyone that the police ended up with that tape recording, otherwise we might never have known what was going on."

Nish looked around, smiling, his right hand raised in a royal wave.

"Thank you," he said. "Thank you very much. Thank you very much."

17

THE SUMMER HOCKEY CAMP WORLD PEEWEE CHAM-
pionship would be a single match, Screech Owls
against Aeros, winner take all. Muck Munro
would be behind the Owls' bench, and Sarah's
father, Mr. Cuthbertson, would handle the Aeros'
bench. Simon and Jason would referee. Starting
centres: Sarah Cuthbertson for the Aeros, Travis
Lindsay for the Screech Owls.

Travis couldn't remember ever feeling quite so
alive before the puck had even dropped. It was
better than before the championship game in
Lake Placid, the big game at the Little Stanley
Cup in Toronto, the fantastic final against the
Waskaganish Wolverines at the First Nations Pee
Wee Hockey Tournament in James Bay. And yet
nothing was at stake here. There were no reporters
in the stands, no scouts, almost no fans. If you
took away the parents, the seats would be completely empty. The game wasn't sanctioned, the
officials weren't real, and the score wouldn't count
for anything but a bit of good-natured ribbing.

But it felt good. It felt absolutely right when
Travis was taping on his shin pads – right one

first, then left – and Muck had walked in and scowled at them. It felt perfect when he'd come in after everyone was dressed and Nish had started holding his gut and bouncing lightly so his head kept dipping down toward his knees. Muck had stood there and waited for everyone's attention, Nish's included. He reminded the forwards to keep to the hash marks in their own end, and the defence not to get caught pinching, and told them all to watch their passes.

Muck was right back where he belonged.

Sarah smiled at Travis just before Simon dropped the puck. It was great to be back playing with Sarah – even if she was on the other team. It was great to be reminded what a beautiful skater she was and what a brilliant playmaker. Travis wished she was still with the Owls, but he understood; she said she was headed for the 2002 Olympics in Salt Lake City, and everyone was absolutely sure she would make it.

The puck dropped, and the roar that burst from the parents was as loud and excited as in any real tournament.

Travis used Sarah's own little trick and plucked the puck out of the air before it hit the ice. He pulled it into his skates, turned so his hip blocked Sarah from checking him, and sent a quick pass back to Nish.

He was sure he heard Nish laugh as he picked up the puck.

Nish waited for Sarah's winger to chase him, then slipped the puck neatly between her skates and bounced a pass off the boards to Derek, who hit Travis at centre.

Travis didn't have to think, didn't even have to look. This, he told himself, is when hockey becomes art. He and Dmitri had worked this play so many times, they could do it in their sleep. He lofted the puck up and past the defence, while Dmitri used his astonishing speed to slip around the defence and get instantly clear. The shoulder fake . . . the Aeros goalie went down . . . and Dmitri roofed a backhand.

Owls 1, Aeros 0.

Travis closed his eyes when he got to the bench. He could feel Muck's big hand on his neck. He could feel Nish smack the seat of his pants with his stick. He could feel Dmitri's shoulder against his, the two of them now so used to each other on the ice that they no longer needed words or even looks to communicate. They just *knew* where each other was, and where each other would be.

Sarah's line had stayed out. She was still smiling. And before the face-off, she skated right along the Owls' bench.

"*Hey, Naked Boy!*" she called out.

Naked Boy? Everyone looked around, wondering what she meant. She was looking directly at Nish. He had his head down, but was watching her suspiciously.

"*What about it, Naked Boy?*" Sarah called. "*No skinny dipping so far?*"

"Tonight," Nish said.

"*Sure,*" Sarah laughed. "*We'll believe it when we see it!*"

"You won't see nothin'," Nish said, shaking his head.

"That's 'cause there's nothing to see!" kidded Sarah.

Simon whistled for the centres to come to centre ice for the face-off, and Sarah skated away, still laughing.

Travis leaned back and said to Nish: "What's this about 'Naked Boy'?"

Nish shook his head. "I have no idea – but it's a great improvement over 'Fat Boy.'"

The game went back and forth for more than an hour. Sarah scored; Gordie Griffith scored on a hard shot from high in the circle; an Aeros defence scored on a deflection; Nish scored on a low shot from the point; Travis scored; and Sarah scored again, on a beautiful solo rush in which she simply skated around poor Wilson and drew Jeremy half out of his net before dropping the puck in over the line.

Owls 4, Aeros 3.

"Last two minutes of play!" Simon shouted before dropping the puck again.

The Owls and Aeros both pulled off quick line changes. Muck wanted Travis's line out, with Nish and Data back on defence. The Aeros, of course, wanted Sarah out. She had scored twice and set up the third of the Aeros' three goals, and she was clearly fired up for this match against her old team and coach.

The ice was bad. Travis hated ice toward the end of the period and late in games. He loved new ice, so freshly flooded it was as if his skates were writing his name on the smooth surface. He liked quick, smooth ice for passing, hard ice for his fast turns, quick ice for his shots. This ice was chopped up and snowy. He could barely carry the puck in it.

Nish had the puck behind his own net, watch-ing, waiting. If he could kill some time, so much the better. The Owls had the lead, after all. But at the very least, he wanted to get the puck out clean so the Owls could take it into the Aeros' end. Sarah Cuthbertson couldn't score from there.

Travis knew his play. He was to skate back hard and turn sharp right in front of his own net. Heading up ice on a slight angle, Nish would either hit him with a direct pass or else fire it out along the boards for either Derek or Dmitri on the wing to chop out past the defence so Travis could pick the puck up in the neutral zone. Travis could then cross centre ice and dump it in.

Travis dug deep and turned. Nish made a fancy play, firing the puck on his backhand so it hit the boards behind him and bounced out just after the forechecking forward had gone by. Nish had time, and he saw Travis. He went for the up-ice pass. He passed hard, and the puck hit the back of Travis's blade perfectly, right at the blueline.

Travis was already in full flight. He looked up immediately to see one defence charging him, chancing a poke check. He tried to do what Nish had done earlier in the game – just slip the puck between the checker's skates. But that had been on good ice, and the ice was now so thick and slow that the puck stopped dead, and the checker had a chance to drag her skate so it picked up the puck.

The Aero kicked the puck ahead to her stick and then hit Sarah Cuthbertson, who was charging back. Sarah turned instantly, actually passing to herself by leaving a drop pass which she then picked up going the other way. Travis couldn't believe how fast she had been able to change from one direction to the other.

There was only Nish back. He was too smart to be fooled again by Sarah's trick of picking up the puck. He wasn't about to lunge; he was going to wait.

Sarah bent as if to scoop the puck again, but Nish refused to go for it. She scooped snow instead, flicking it in the air at Nish's head. He instinctively ducked, and when he moved slightly, Sarah dropped the puck into her skates, knocked it from one blade to the other and then back up onto her stick, which was already on the other side of Nish.

A quick wrist shot, and all Travis could see was the net bulge behind Jeremy.

Sarah had tied the game: Owls 4, Aeros 4.

The Aeros leapt from the bench and jumped all over Sarah. Simon blew his whistle, and the game was over. A tie. The best result possible. The parents rose in a standing ovation. Muck raced across the ice and shook Mr. Cuthbertson's hand, the two of them laughing at what they had just seen.

The two teams lined up to shake hands. Travis followed Nish, who seemed heartbroken that he had let Sarah slip away.

"C'mon, you owed her one," Travis said.

"I guess."

They came to Sarah, who had her helmet off and was still laughing.

"Now you know why we call you 'Naked Boy,'" she said to Nish.

"I don't get it," he said.

"I just undressed you out there, didn't I?"

18

"I'M DOING IT."

Travis had never seen such determination on his friend's face.

"I'm doing it," Nish repeated.

Tomorrow they would be going home. They had just had the big end-of-camp dinner, both teams present, and special awards had been given to Sarah Cuthbertson, for Most Valuable Player, and to Travis, much to his surprise, for Most Valuable Camper. He had a suspicion that Muck had come up with this one on his own. Before Muck could announce the winner, the entire gathering had risen to their feet to honour Muck with long, loud, spontaneous applause.

They would end this extraordinary week at hockey camp with a marshmallow roast and a moonlight swim.

"I'm going to do it."

It was a beautiful night. The parents had built a huge bonfire down by the shore, and it sparked and roared, lighting up the entire beach and halfway out to the diving platform at the end of the dock. The stars were out, big and bright and too many even to begin counting. Someone pointed out Orion. Everyone thought of Mr. Clifford, and how sad it was that such a kind, interesting man could have ended up a murderer.

They toasted marshmallows. Data amazed the entire gathering by burning his marshmallows until they were like pieces of black coal, and then biting them whole off the end of his toasting stick. Nish amazed everyone by eating somewhere between fifty and a hundred of them. Some of them he didn't even wait to toast.

It wasn't Nish showing off, Travis knew. It was nerves.

"I'm still going to do it," he said when they were all gathered around the fire. One of the parents had brought a guitar, and a singsong was starting up.

The Screech Owls and Aeros were starting to swim. Sarah was first off the diving platform, and she swam out in the dark, black water and turned on her back. "*Any Nish sightings?*" she called.

"*None!*"

"*Pssst!*"

Travis turned just as he was about to dive off the end of the dock. He could barely make Nish out in the shadows.

"*Over here! C'm'ere!*"

Travis hurried in under the diving platform, where Nish was huddled with Andy. Even in the dim light, Travis could see Nish was shivering. And it wasn't a cold evening.

"Y-you two are m-my witnesses, okay?" Nish said.

"Okay," Andy said.

"*You're really going to do it?*" said Travis.

"Just watch!"

Quick as a flash, Nish dropped his bathing trunks. He dived off the dock, and swam deep under the water, as far out as he could go.

But when he came up, he was screaming.

"TTTTUUUUUURRTTTTLLLE!!!!!!"

Travis couldn't believe his eyes. The water around Nish was foaming as he flailed away. Still screaming, Nish raced for the dock, his arms thrashing desperately in the water.

Halfway back, he stopped, reached down into the water, and shrieked.

"HHHELLLPPPPPP MMMEEEEE!"

Andy and Travis raced to the end of the dock as Nish approached, his flailing arms splashing them both. He reached up, still screaming.

"HE GRABBED ME!! THE TURTLE GRABBED MY TOE!!!"

Others were screaming now and racing to get out. Travis couldn't believe it. Had Mr. Clifford lied to them about snapping turtles? He'd said they'd never attack.

Nish used his friends' outstretched arms to pull himself up and clear of the water.

He reached under the diving platform for his bathing suit. *It was gone!*

"NNNNNNOOOOOOOOOOOO!!!" Nish screamed.

Covering himself with his hands, Nish took off. Stark naked, he ran the length of the dock and onto the shore, past the singsong, which had come to a sudden halt, and up the path to the cabins, screaming all the way.

"NNNNNNNNNNNOOOOOOOOOOOOOOOOOOO!!!"

"*Go, Naked Boy!*"

Sarah was in the water at the end of the dock. She had a scuba mask and snorkel pulled up off her face.

Sarah, the snapping turtle.

She reached out, and someone behind Andy and Travis threw her a pair of dark bathing trunks.

They turned. It was Liz Moscovitz and Jennie Staples. They must have swiped Nish's trunks when Andy and Travis were "witnessing" Nish's skinny dip.

Laughing, Sarah held Nish's bathing suit above her head.

"*This* trophy I'm keeping," she said. "You hit somebody from behind, you're going pay for it!"

In the distance, Travis was sure he heard a screen door slam. And then the inside door.

And even then, he could still make out the call of the Nishikawa.

"NNNNNNNNNNNNOOOOOOOOOOOOOOOOOOO!!!"

THE FIRST BOOK IN THE SCREECH OWLS SERIES

Mystery at Lake Placid

Travis Lindsay, his best friend, Nish, and all their pals on the Screech Owls hockey team, are on their way to New York State for an international peewee tournament. Excitement builds in the team van on their way to Lake Placid. First there are the entertaining antics of their trainer, Mr. Dillinger – then there's the prospect of playing on an Olympic rink, in a huge arena, knowing there will be scouts in the stands.

But they have barely arrived when things start to go wrong. Their star player, Sarah, plays badly from lack of sleep. Next Travis gets knocked down in the street. And then someone starts tampering with their equipment. It looks as if someone is trying to sabotage the Screech Owls. But who? And why? And can Travis and the others stop the destruction before the decisive game of the tournament?

THE SECOND BOOK IN THE SCREECH OWLS SERIES

The Night They Stole the Stanley Cup

Someone is out to steal the Stanley Cup – and only the Screech Owls stand between the thieves and their prize!

Travis, Nish, and the rest of the Screech Owls have come to Toronto for the biggest hockey tournament of their lives – only to find themselves in the biggest *mess* of their lives. First Nish sprains his ankle falling down the stairs at the CN Tower. Later, key members of the team get caught shoplifting. And during a tour of the Hockey Hall of Fame, Travis overhears two men plotting to swipe the priceless Stanley Cup and hold it for ransom!

Can the Screech Owls do anything to save the most revered trophy in the land? And can the team also rise to the challenge on the ice and play their best hockey ever?

THE THIRD BOOK IN THE SCREECH OWLS SERIES

The Screech Owls' Northern Adventure

The Screech Owls are on the road again, on a bumpy plane ride way up North that will land them in some very deep trouble!

When Jesse Highboy's dad asked the Screech Owls how they felt about going to James Bay to play in the First Nations Pee Wee Hockey Tournament, everyone thought it was a great idea.

It was the first time a non-native team had been invited, and the pressure would be on the Owls to live up to the honour and play some good clean hockey. More important, Travis and his teammates would also get the chance to stay with local native families, eat traditional food, travel by Ski-Doo, and experience what life in the North is all about.

But freezing to death all alone in the bush, with a storm howling and the dreaded Trickster stalking the night? No one had asked the Screech Owls how they felt about that!

Mystery at Lake Placid
The Night They Stole the Stanley Cup
The Screech Owls' Northern Adventure
Murder at Hockey Camp
Kidnapped in Sweden
Terror in Florida
The Quebec City Crisis
The Screech Owls' Home Loss
Nightmare in Nagano